The Queens's Heart
The Growing Strong Series
Book 2

Michel Prince

Published by
Satin Romance
An Imprint of Melange Books, LLC
White Bear Lake, MN 55110
www.satinromance.com

ISBN: 978-1-68046-343-9

Cover Design by Ashley Byland from Redbird Designs

The Queen's Heart is for all the moms that ever felt they failed. Thank you to my fans for supporting my books, my husband and son for giving me time to write them and my editor Kyle for making them shine.
Special thanks to Isaac Hernandez and Heather Mae for translation help.

One loyal friend is worth ten thousand relatives.
-Euripides

Chapter One

"Life's hard. It's even harder when you're stupid."
—John Wayne

With a loud thwack the mini soccer ball Luke had gotten from his father made contact with the back of his mother's head.

"Lucas Nathan Wallace!"

Mary Beth Wallace rarely pulled out the full name on her son. Even though she knew it had been an accident, she was fried. It'd been a long day and all she could think about was all she'd given up. All she'd gone through. All her friends had gone through to support the two of them. She knew Luke was only five, but damn it, she was not a soccer goal— she was a human being, even if she hadn't felt that way in years.

Mary Beth had already been stumbling up the stairs to her apartment as she tried not to drop her groceries while Luke straggled behind her. She should have known to position him in front of her.

It was the fighting and then forgiving with Luke's father that kept her off balance. She knew better than to let Nate get to her with his strange demands and light blue eyes.

"Sorry, Mama." Luke's sweet voice strengthened her.

"No, I'm sorry. Just pick up your ball and let's get home before I drop the groceries."

Luke picked up his ball and she sighed as he bounded up the stairs. As they turned the corner to Mary Beth's apartment, number twelve, a man she'd never seen before bumped her shoulder. The groceries she'd placed in a paper bag tore from her arm, causing boxed and canned food to roll toward the stairs.

"Oh my God, I'm so sorry," the man said as he practically dove at the stairs to catch the cans before they bounced down the steps. "I've made a dozen trips and only bumped into my brothers helping me out," he explained as he stacked the cans. "I'm moving into sixteen."

Just what Mary Beth needed—another man knocking her off balance and messing up her life.

"Here, Mama." Luke had three cans overflowing his little arms, reminding her she wasn't going to be a man hating bitch, at least where her son could see it. She'd never want to make him feel less than human because she'd messed up.

"It's okay, I probably would have dropped the bag when I got my keys out."

Mary Beth unlocked her apartment and placed the three plastic bags she had on the other arm inside the door. Luke continued to help gather the groceries from the floor with the dark haired stranger.

"I'm Elias," he said, extending his hand. "You can call me Eli if you want."

"Mary Beth," she replied, crossing her arms.

"*Oso chiquito*," another slightly older looking, dark haired stranger barked and berated Eli as he passed. "*No tenemos tiempo en lo que tu te acuestas con todo el mundo.*"

Eli replied in Spanish, and Mary Beth wished she hadn't taken German in high school. "Sorry about that."

Two more Hispanic guys passed giving Eli and Mary Beth annoyed glares.

"It sucks being one of the youngest sometimes." He pulled back his hand and placed the fallen groceries just inside the door. "I see you have a professional soccer player with you."

"That'd be my son, Luke."

"Nice to meet you."

"Hello, sir," Luke replied with a small shake of the hand.

"You can call me Eli."

"Okay, Eli, sir." Luke quickly made his escape as he ducked inside.

"It's a quiet floor, I'm sure you'll like it here."

"I hope so. If everyone's as forgiving as you."

If Mary Beth hadn't been mad she'd have noticed how his black tank top clung to his torso as sweat glistened against his deeply tanned skin. Although he did have larger biceps, his stomach had a little paunch to it. The men she knew who never obsessed over that area of their body always made her feel more comfortable because they'd never let her down. His thick, black hair stuck out from under a tattered Twins cap, and he had long, black lashes surrounding his obsidian eyes. In another time or place Mary Beth would have taken a second look, but today she just wanted to make supper and crash for five minutes before doing homework.

"If you need anything, just knock," she said for some unknown reason. "Softly, if it's after eight. That's when Luke goes to bed."

"Thank you, Mary...Beth." Eli smiled as he walked backward and tripped on the first step. "I'm not a bumbling fool, usually."

"Uh huh."

Mary Beth entered her small apartment to find that her son had dragged the groceries into their little galley kitchen. Her apartment also had two bedrooms, or a bedroom and what to her seemed like a really big closet that Luke slept in, but it was hers and she'd done it on her own.

Between work and Nate, a dull ache had formed behind Mary Beth's right eye, making her wish a shower and bed were in her near future. But she was a mom and moms had to cook supper and get their kid to bed before they start on their own studies.

"How about spaghetti?"

"Again," Luke grumbled as he pulled himself up on one of the stools at the island across from the stove.

"Again? We haven't had spaghetti since...Monday. It was just on Monday wasn't it big guy?"

"Yep."

With it being Wednesday, she would have to get creative. Mac and cheese was out since they had that last night. Chicken nuggets it was. Dang, she was hoping to make those on Saturday as a treat. After a "well-balanced" meal of nuggets, peas, and French fries, Luke was bathed and put to bed.

3

Powering up her laptop, Mary Beth logged into the chat rooms for the classes at the local community college. An hour, three ibuprofen, and a half a pint of pistachio ice cream later, she was distracted by a light tapping on her door.

Peeking through the peephole she saw a mound of matted down black hair.

"Hello?"

"Hey Mary, it's me Eli. I didn't wake Luke did I?"

Mary Beth opened the door a crack to see him smiling at her.

"No."

"Good. Hey, three of my light bulbs have burnt out. I'm practically in the dark. You wouldn't have a few lying around? I could pick you up some tomorrow when I'm at work."

"You work at a light bulb store?"

"No, a bank, but we're in Cub so you know picking up something is easy for me."

"Let me look."

Mary Beth let him in, closed the door, and cocked her head to the side. What a strange request at almost ten at night. Digging under her sink she found a package with two bulbs and passed them to Eli.

"Thanks, you're the only person who's talked to me since I've moved in."

"It's only been a few hours."

"Yeah, I guess. I have some left over pizza if you're interested?"

Mary Beth could not understand how one man could talk so much.

"You know, moving day necessity. It was either that or sliders and I didn't think breaking in my toilet was the way I wanted to move."

And now she was totally weirded out.

"My friends were all working and I needed to get out of my old place...look at me not giving you a second to say boo."

Hitching her thumb over her shoulder she said, "I have to get back to work."

"You work from home? That is so nice. You know, my sister would love to work from home."

"Okay, Eli, I have school work to finish."

"You're in college. Where?"

4

"Stop. I don't want to be rude, but...breathe."

"Yeah," Eli backed up and gave a meek shrug with his shoulders. "I'm sorry, it's just..."

"I'm the only female that's ever talked to you."

"No. You're just the prettiest one."

She studied him for a moment and crossed her arms. "Are you really in the dark?"

"Yes, that's true. I was glad I had an excuse, but you can check if you want...but you probably don't." Eli let out a large gust of air. "I'll leave, thanks for the light bulbs, I'll leave the ones I buy by the door. I won't bother you again."

As Mary Beth closed her door on her very strange new neighbor she heard him call out.

"I'm in sixteen...if you...you know...want to borrow...never mind."

* * * *

Eli wondered what the hell just happened to him as he closed the door to his new apartment. He had never lost his ability to filter his thoughts when talking to a girl who he found attractive. He'd turn on the Latin charm passed down from generations of Marquez men that had created more babies then he could count. Especially with a *güera*. They always liked when he used his slight accent.

Mary Beth had surprised him. She had let him in her apartment after ten at night. After replacing the bulbs, he continued unpacking hand-me-downs from his older brothers and sister.

The fourth of five children, Eli was used to getting most things third hand. His mother would buy his older brother Eddie's clothes a little too big and pass Carlos and him belts. Only his sister Angelica got brand new everything. She didn't even have to have his mother's hand-me downs like the boys did with their father. Eli's only solace was he'd be dumping the crap on his brother Jesus in a few years when, like his older brothers and sisters, he'd established his home and could buy new.

He made his bed with the canary yellow sheets that probably were a gift at his parent's wedding and crashed. Even with three brothers helping, the move had worn him out.

"Yeah," Eli answered his phone.

"So," his little brother teased. "That red head that made you think you didn't have to do any heavy lifting."

"I knocked her groceries out of her hands. You want me to get an assault charge my first day in the building?"

"I just want to be able to bring my girl by your place and not have competition for the bed."

"There's not enough plastic sheeting in the world that would allow you to screw on my bed."

"Ah, come on. Carlos and Eddie are married. You're the only one with your own place now."

"Yes, and I earned it."

Working hard to get his degree while helping his family with bills when his father hurt his leg. They all helped out, but he had to keep the house up at the same time.

"Whatever, how about that second bedroom?"

"You know that's for Gloria and David and if you soil their room, I'll castrate you."

"Where am I supposed to take my girl?"

"Church."

"Come on, Eli," Jesus whined.

"You're sixteen. Get a job. save some money, buy a car, and take her to a lake."

"You're destroying my high school existence."

"Then I've done my job as your older brother."

"This sucks."

Eli hung up the phone and thought again about Mary Beth's green speckled hazel eyes and fire red hair. Normally he loved long, flowing locks, but Mary Beth's was cute, cut short in a pixie style. He hated to be such a man about things, but she was his height, maybe an inch taller. Eli could already hear the jokes about that from his brothers. *Look at Eli and Helga the Wonder Wife.* Of course with how long her legs were...man, he wanted those wrapped around his waist in the most unnatural of ways.

* * * *

Mary Beth started her day by changing her clothes after spilling scalding coffee on her pants. With what she assumed bordered on a second-degree burn, she somehow managed to get Luke buckled into his booster seat and herself into the car with five minutes to spare.

Sadly, five minutes wasn't enough. When she turned the key in her ignition she got nothing—not a rrrrrr, not a sputter, not even a click.

"Why! Why! Why!" she said as she shook the steering wheel. It was only five-thirty, but she had no other option.

"Hello," Maury's groggy voice answered her call. "Who is this?"

"I'm so sorry, Mr. Vaulst."

"Mary Beth? That you? What's the problem?"

"I hate to ask again, but I think it's my starter or battery. I don't know. Is there any chance you could bring me to work, then look at my car today?"

Maury, her best friend Gabbie Thomas' father, to all her friends relief, was a pretty good mechanic. Even though he had his own shop, he shade treed it for his daughter and her friends quite a bit.

"All right, give me fifteen minutes and I'll get you to work. You opening today?"

"Yes, with Sarah."

Ten minutes later while Luke finished the toast and banana she'd given him as breakfast, Maury pulled up.

"There's my Lukey boy," Maury said as Luke rushed out of the minivan into the arms of his pseudo grandpa.

Since Mary Beth's parents still didn't acknowledge her or Luke after they kicked her out, Maury had stepped in as Grandpa. The "get the hell out of my house" from her mother was a fine how-do-you-do to give a seventeen-year-old who was already freaking out. Her mother had seen Mary Beth's pregnancy as an attempt to embarrass her publicly. Mary Beth knew she'd be mad, but they'd been close, so Mary Beth never in a million years thought she'd be tossed out like gutter trash.

"It's that damn tramp Mandy you're always around. She has no father and her mother's a slut. How else would an unmarried woman get pregnant? Maybe one of your whore friends will help you, because we won't."

At first Mary Beth thought her parents just needed a cooling off period. Six years later, she still hadn't spoken to her parents or siblings. The pictures she'd sent of Luke the first year were returned unopened.

"Luke, you eating spark plugs again?" Maury teased as he drove the two of them to the Growing Strong Montessori Day Care Center.

Thanks to Luke's unexpected conception, Mary Beth had decided to forgo her partial scholarship and raise him. To her surprise her friends did too. Together they purchased an established daycare center. Sure her friends told her it wasn't like they had full rides, but still, she had guilt over the three of them joining in her bad mistake.

Over the past few years the name had changed and the Montessori was added as Gabbie, Sarah, and Mandy began their Montessori training, and now their little business at the end of a strip mall was bustling with children.

Sarah had her ash-blonde hair pulled back in a ponytail, as usual. Standing at the front desk, she greeted the early parents as they dropped their kids off and tucked items into the cubbies. Jasmine, a newer employee, was setting out some juice and breakfast bars for the kids in the Children's House level classroom when Mary Beth finally came in with Luke. He rushed to put his green backpack away and quickly found his little buddy Max violently stabbing a juice box in vain with its straw. The bell over the door rang and Mary Beth turned to see Maury.

"I need the keys, kiddo."

"Right." Mary Beth fumbled in her purse and tossed him the keys.

"If I can get it fixed before Gabbie leaves I'll have her drive it in for you," Maury said.

"Thank you."

"Car broke again?" Sarah asked as Mary Beth took her place on the stool to greet parents.

"It's a day ending in Y isn't it? I'm so fed up with that darn thing."

"Are you here all day?"

"I've got a class at ten, eleven, and noon, but I should be back by two. Why?"

"Just wondering if you wanted to have lunch now that your little buddy goes to school."

"How do I have a kid old enough for school?" Mary Beth balked. "Seriously? I swear I don't even understand it. I'm used to putting the older kids on the bus, but my own…"

"I'm more interested in turning the center into a school so he doesn't have to leave us."

"Yes, I'm sure it's because you don't want Luke to leave," Mary Beth teased her friend.

Mary Beth's current project at work was to get the paperwork in order and register them as an official school with the state. Ever since Gabbie learned about the Montessori method, all four of them wanted to move away from changing diapers to raising leaders. It was the first thing that made them change the name of the center to Growing Strong.

"I'm used to the little demon spawn. Speaking of which, please say you spent less than two minutes picking him up yesterday."

Aw crap, she was caught. Sarah was the current president of the 'I hate Nate the Ass Munch Club'. True, Mary Beth founded it one dark afternoon, but she'd eased up and well…although she wished she didn't still have feelings for him, she did.

"See, what happened was—"

"Oh, let me guess, Luke was napping and it took Nate two minutes to talk you out of your pants, two minutes to do whatever it is you heteros find satisfying, and then Luke woke up."

"Worse."

"One minute?" Sarah's eyebrow raised.

"Carrie had taken Luke for ice cream," Mary Beth said meekly.

"You tramp. His poor, unassuming wife was caring for your child while you…"

Holding up her hand and closing her eyes in shame Mary Beth shook her head. "Stop, I already want to vomit."

"As long as you're not carrying more demon spawn, fine. I'd need to cleanse my pallet too if Nate touched me."

"You know, you never liked him."

"Preach on."

"What are we preaching about today?" Mandy asked as she sauntered in all sex and candy as usual.

How she could look like sex on a platter in the standard uniform of khakis and a black polo with their logo of a child placing the last piece on the pink tower, Mary Beth would never understand. Mandy just had a way about her with her flawless olive coloring, long black hair, and hazel eyes with chestnut brown speckles in them.

"Nate had Luke after school yesterday for a few hours," Sarah explained.

"Nap time again?" Mandy asked as she tossed her backpack into Mary Beth's office.

"You have a locker."

"I'm part owner, I should have an office."

"Offices are for people who do things."

"I do things, I'm a…" Mandy cocked her head to the side and looked at Sarah. "What title did Gabbie give us again?"

"Lead Young Life Specialist."

"Yeah, what she said."

They had finally been able to hire three full time and four-part time employees to help with general care of the children. This allowed Mandy, Gabbie, and Sarah to run classrooms as opposed to straight babysitting. Mary Beth's job was the business end. Although she did her own share of classroom help, she hadn't taken all the early childhood certifications the rest of the employees had.

"Sarah preaching about leaving the man alone?" Mandy asked, sadly remembering the initial conversation.

"No, that she hates him."

"Oh, preach on," Mandy said with her hand raised as if she were in a gospel choir. "List the sins of the fallen Catholic angel."

Mandy always got a kick out of Sarah when she would go into a rant, especially if alcohol was involved. Today, luckily there was none and parents would be coming in soon, hopefully cutting the conversation short.

"You know what, I have kids to check in and you two need to find your classrooms."

"You can kick us out, but even if you cover all the mirrors you'll still have to face yourself," Sarah said as she and Mandy went to find the kids in their classrooms. "I mean is it that good?" she mumbled to Mandy.

"Not his, but some men are worth it."

The thought of Eli's long lashes and dark eyes jumped into Mary Beth's head. Right, the nonstop talker two doors down, that's who she needed in her life. Not.

Chapter Two

The truth is you don't know what is going to happen tomorrow. Life is a crazy ride, and nothing is guaranteed.

—Eminem

Eli's alarm was a blaring reminder that he was an adult. Three snooze taps and finally a fist silenced the screeching bitch making him miss his mother gently bringing him coffee. Coffee. Damn. He forgot all about unpacking his coffee maker last night. He'd have to motivate himself this morning. So not...wait a minute. Mary Beth might have some coffee.

The Southern half of his body came awake at the idea of his fire haired, sexy neighbor. Eli stumbled to the bathroom and ran a comb through his hair. A little stubble in the morning was acceptable since he would be begging for a warm cup of go-go juice. Flashing his winning smile, he made his way to apartment twelve.

Knocking a few times with no response he wandered back to his apartment. Turning the handle, he felt no give and realized he'd forgot to leave the door unlocked. Shit. Standing in his pajama bottoms and tank top he was completely locked out. The office for the building wouldn't be open until a half hour after he was due at work.

Returning to Mary Beth's apartment he knocked again, a little more vigorously.

"What are you, the police coming for a raid?" the muffled voice of an older man grumbled. "I heard you the last time, can't a man take a few minutes to himself?"

When the door opened a man in his fifties held an econ textbook and glared at him. He had a small potbelly and the shorter man's gray hair was rumpled in back as if he'd been wearing a hat not that long ago.

"Why are you beating down Mary Beth's door?" he asked with a scowl.

"I...I...um...sir...see..."

"Spit it out, I don't have all morning."

"Mary's—"

"Mary Beth."

"Right, sorry, Mary Beth's the only one I know in the building—"

"Then you should know most mornings she's gone by five-thirty."

"I just moved in and..."

"You lock yourself out?"

"Yeah, how did you know?"

"Mary Beth did that at least three times a week when she first moved in here. Give me a minute to get my tools from her car and I'll pop it."

"You're a locksmith?"

"Nope, just a master criminal."

Eli blanched at the comment and the old man shook his head at him.

"You look like you could use a cup of coffee. I needed one too, but I can't finish the whole pot myself. I was just about to throw it out. Here, come in and I'll give you one."

"Thanks, that's actually why I came here. I forgot to unpack my pot last night—"

The man raised his hand, stopping what was going to be the second day of Eli's inability to shut his trap.

"Not because you were hoping Mary Beth was single?" the man asked with an arched eyebrow.

"No, she was just really nice yesterday and I'm sorry I didn't introduce myself. I'm Elias Marquez. You can call me Eli."

"Maury," he said as he firmly shook Eli's hand.

Eli went in the kitchen and poured the now unnecessary cup of coffee. After a deep whiff of the dark brown liquid Eli tried not to be rude. He could tell without tasting the quality of Mary Beth's coffee would leave much to be desired. With Maury fetching tools, Eli took time to look around Mary Beth's apartment. It seemed smaller than his, but then again, she had it unpacked. Her home was practically spotless with only a cup and knife in the sink to be washed. On her walls were pictures of Luke from birth to now. She had a collage with pictures of her with three other girls in different poses. Some looked to be from grade and high school, while others seemed much more recent since Luke was on her hip. She was a softball player, or at least she used to be, and at one time she had long, flowing, garnet colored hair.

"One of the best pitchers in the local leagues." Maury's voice made Eli jump.

"Who are the other girls?"

"The Growing Strong Mafia." He chuckled. "Or at least that's what my son-in-law calls them."

Son-in-law. Damn, Maury must be Mary Beth's dad, although Eli couldn't see the resemblance. It was the only thing that made sense. Mary Beth must have a husband. Double damn. So much for his chance at hitting the jackpot with his new neighbor.

Maury crossed to the picture and pointed to a blond. "That's Sarah, she plays third, next to her is Mandy, she's first base, you know Mary Beth, and finally Gabbie, the catcher."

"Why are they called a mafia? Is it because of your profession?"

"My profession? No, theirs. They all own the Growing Strong Day Care down on McKnight and tend to be overprotective of each other." Maury picked up the cup of coffee he'd left on the counter and finished the last of it. "I'm a mechanic, son, and the locks in this building are cheap so keep the chain on when you're...sorry I'm used to a room full of girls. Thank God for my grandson or I'd be overwhelmed by estrogen."

"I wouldn't know. I have one sister and a niece. Otherwise it's men as far as the eye can see at our house."

"You come from a big family then?"

"Five."

The door flung open and the dark haired girl from the pictures burst into the apartment.

"Yo, I need the keys, I'm already late."

"All right, all right. It's not like you own the place…wait, Gabbert, you do. Calm down."

"Who's this?" the woman snapped. "You let a stranger in Mary Beth's apartment?"

"This is her neighbor, Eli. He got locked out. I was just helping him with his door."

"From Mary Beth's kitchen. You're better than I thought." The sarcastic tone she took with him would have gotten Eli a slap to the back of his head as a child. Who was he kidding, it still would get him a slap.

"Keys." He tossed them at Gabbie. "Don't forget her econ book. She needs it for class today."

Gabbie snagged the book and gave Eli a cold stare. A chill ran down his spine as he quickly understood the mafia comment. He stayed silent until she left, afraid to poke the bear.

"What apartment is yours?" Maury asked and they headed to Eli's.

"How many bodies have they buried?" he asked Maury while he worked on his door.

"Too many to count. Gabbie's softened since she got married. You should have seen her before. Especially when it came to Luke. If only Mary Beth would let them loose on his father, we could all have peace."

"Luke's father's a bad guy?"

"Guy would insinuate he was a man at some time in his life." A small crack sounded and Eli's door opened.

"If you really are becoming friends with Mary Beth maybe you two could swap keys so I don't have to come over here to break you guys in anymore."

"Are you sure that would be appropriate?"

"Since when do kids these days worry about appearances? It was just an idea. It wouldn't matter, with that darn P.O.S. she drives I'll still be here three times a week."

"You were here for her car?"

"It wasn't for the coffee, blech, that girl has no understanding of dark roast."

Eli laughed. Her coffee had to be a store brand. A cheap store brand.

"Next time I'll have my coffee pot going and you can get some good Kahona beans."

15

"These girls don't understand there are some things you don't skimp on. Sure they'll splurge on double ply toilet paper, but a good cup of Joe? Nope. It was nice to meet you Eli."

"You too, sir."

"Awe, call me Maury."

"Will do, Maury."

Eli showered, dressed, and got to work with a few minutes to spare. If nothing else, it gave him time to pick up some light bulbs.

* * * *

"So, who is he?" Gabbie asked as she stood in the doorway of Mary Beth's office.

"Who's who?" she responded as she saved the spreadsheet she had up.

"The new neighbor," Gabbie replied with a glint in her eye. "He's pretty cute."

"Aren't you married?"

"Yep, happily. But I wasn't six months ago, so spill it."

"You didn't look at guys a year ago, you know."

"Ah well, love is in the air."

"Thanks for reminding me. I'll make sure to call the guys to clean out the duct work." Mary Beth waved her pen in the air.

"Would you quit playing coy and spill."

"How did you meet my neighbor?" Mary Beth's eyebrows knitted together as strange worlds were colliding.

"He was drinking coffee with my dad when I picked up your keys this morning."

Mary Beth turned in her chair and crossed her arms.

"Was he chatting up a storm?" she half joked since it seemed Eli couldn't stop talking the night before.

"We're talking my father, with a guy."

"How did you get a word in?"

"Oh, you know. Snapped them to attention, got what I needed and left."

"He moved in yesterday. He seems nice."

"Nice or *nice?*" Gabbie teased.

Mary Beth revisited her few minutes with Eli and, for some reason, she felt heat rising in a variety of places. He did have a great smile and his nervousness was actually adorable.

"Wow, silence and red face. Could Mary Beth have actually dreamed about someone other than Nathan last night?"

She did wake up with a hand between her thighs...and Elias was handsome and did smell really good when he came into her apartment. Mary Beth shook the idea from her head.

"I don't dream about Nate, unless you count nightmares."

If nothing else, Nate's name could calm down any excitement that might have been building between her legs.

"I heard Nate picked up Luke from school yesterday."

"Oh, my, God. You get laid on the regular, why do you care?"

"You think any of us are jealous of you having bad sex with Nate?"

"You know what, it's my life. I don't owe you guys anything. You chose to stay here and I...I..."

"How about me? The one whose office you were crying in because of Nate last spring? Or Mandy, who took you to the batting cage for six hours when he got married? What about Sarah, who has picked you up a hundred times off your bed after taking care of Luke because you were too depressed? Mary Beth, we don't care if you're reading a book with Nate or swinging from a damn trapeze in his bedroom, as long as you don't feel like dog shit afterward."

Mary Beth bit back her tears of frustration. They didn't get it. If she could just get Nate to pull together with her and Luke as a family, then she wouldn't be such a failure. This stupid dream, wish or personal torture, depending on the day, was what created the loop of failure in her mind.

"You guys never understood what Nate and I have."

"Does he? He married another woman. He never needs to commit to you because he has a lifelong commitment to you through Luke. Have you ever said no to him?"

Once, she thought, just once when he demanded she abort Luke. Why hadn't her good Catholic morals stopped her at sex instead of abortion?

"I say no sometimes."

17

"Mary Beth, you went from being his woman to being the other woman. That's not you, that's never been you. Look, I'll tell the other girls to drop it." Gabbie sighed and shook her head. "It's just really hard to see you do this to yourself."

"I'm trying. I really am." Mary Beth ran her fingers through her hair and shook out the negative thoughts running amuck in her mind. "Can we talk business?"

"Do I need to pull Mandy and Sarah from recess duty?" Gabbie hitched her thumb.

"No, let them bask in the fall sun while we have it. I want your opinion first, since you're the education director. If we really want to make the jump into being certified, we need to look at a new facility. Unless we want to just stay with Children's House level learning."

Gabbie closed the door to the office and flopped in the chair.

"Can we afford a new building? I mean the location and rent here is good. How big are we talking?"

"I don't know. How are your contacts at the training center coming? Are people already with schools or looking for jobs?"

Over the last few years they'd hired from the training center with the expectation the Montessori trainees would be helping form a new school.

"It's a mix. But we'll want at least thirty kids per room and I'm not sure if we can do more than one at each level to start with. What happens if we take off? Do we move again?"

"I'd rather have a floor of unused rooms we could expand to than move every few years. I don't think we should rent."

"Buy? A whole building? That changes everything doesn't it? We'd have maintenance issues and if we remodeled, that'd be an issue."

This was why she was talking with Gabbie alone first.

"But we could remodel, unlike here. And there wouldn't be any surprises like 'oh, we decided to up your rent by a grand with only a month's notice' either."

"You're the money woman. We'll trust you."

"I think we need to send out a survey or something to our parents to see if they would even want to stay with us instead of going to public school."

"At least we'd have three kids for sure."

"Yes, but Claire, Charlie, and Luke do not even constitute a classroom, let alone a whole school."

"True, maybe Claire and Charlie need some siblings." Gabbie grinned.

"You're pregnant? Already?"

"No, no," her friend admonished as she waved her hand a few times. "Bite your tongue. It's in discussion. You know Case's parents had problems conceiving and intellectually he knows we're two different people…and Charlie and Claire are our kids in every sense of the word, but still…"

"You want to have a piece of the two of you."

"I'm sure it's a few years off, but still, it's in the air."

"Well now I will keep my legs crossed. Luke needs a brother or sister as much as I need another hole in my head."

"If that's all it took to get you to drop Nate, I'd have talked babies a long time ago."

Chapter Three

Life is ten percent what you make it, and ninety percent how you take it.
—Irving Berlin

While Eli was working he found himself becoming distracted by any flash of red hair. He never knew there were so many shade variations. The strawberry blondes all the way to the electric, fire truck red dye jobs on the more questionable clients. Mary Beth's, he'd determined, was natural—she had the telltale pale skin with lighter freckling. Not a bunch, just a few on her cheekbones. Maybe a few others in soft and sensitive places.

"Stop it," he grumbled under his breath as he inputted a car loan. "Married remember, jackass."

The customer had gone out into the store to shop since he told them pulling credit, entering info, and checking references could take up to thirty minutes. It didn't, he just hated having the nervous applicant sitting across from him bouncing their knee and questioning every keystroke. He understood the nerves. He just didn't want to deal with them.

Why'd he have to bump into Mary Beth the first day? He could have had a month's worth of living in a peaceful abyss. Maybe he could've even met her husband first. That would have been a better way to meet Mary Beth. The locked down status would have been written all over her and he wouldn't have thought twice about his sexy neighbor.

Her legs just didn't stop. And that awkward smile she gave him. Even exhausted, her hazel eyes seemed to be set off with specks of green. She was cautious, as a good mother should be with a strange man, yet open to the opportunity…no, he thought to himself, she was being a

20

neighbor, not inviting him in for a hot date. Geez, what had happened to him? Maybe his brothers were right. He sees a woman and thinks of only one thing.

"Is it ready?" the customer poked her head into the cramped office.

"Almost," he lied and realized it wasn't every woman.

"What's holding it up? I know I don't have much collateral, but surely—"

"It's not you," he assured, holding up his hand to stop the tirade of excuses. "Some agencies run slower on Mondays."

"But it's Tuesday."

"It is?" He looked at the daily calendar in front of him to see it was, in fact, Tuesday. Almost a full week had passed since he moved in and last seen Mary Beth. Casually, he tapped his mouse and his computer beeped. "Last thing I needed, have a seat Ms. Cass."

Eli fumbled through the loan and eventually found her a seven and a half percent interest rate, which, given her credit, was amazing. Luckily, the car she was buying from her third cousin or something was worth the five grand she was paying for it. Most people went to one of the branch offices to fill out loans, but there were just enough wanting to do it in between picking up dinner so he'd been assigned to the store.

It was convenient for him as well when he still lived at home. His mother was notorious for calling him multiple times during the day. He still kept a pack of lined sticky notes on his desk for the daily run through the store. Considering he'd eaten a bowl of dry cereal for the second day in a row, because he'd forgotten to get milk, he'd have to start remembering to do that for himself now.

Maybe he'd call his mother and swing by after work with David and Gloria. She loved seeing her grandkids. Dialing her number, he hoped she'd answer and not...

"Oh, you remembered you have a family."

"Hello, Jesus, what's the matter now?"

"Besides the fact I'm stuck with all the chores—"

"At least there's only three of you now, not four. Although cleaning up after you made it seem like twelve."

"Ha, ha. What do you want?"

21

"I was going to come by and was wondering if mom needs anything."

"Ma!" Jesus yelled, but didn't move the phone far enough away from his mouth. "Elias wants to know if he should pick something up."

"You could have just brought her the phone."

"Well, yeah, but that would have required me to move."

"In that case, I completely understand your reluctance."

"Thank you for your compassion."

"The only reason I'm showing it is because I know you're on the other line, Mama."

"Oh…I can never get anything past you two boys," his mother sighed. "Jesus, stop being a smart butt."

"Yes, Mama."

"Now, hang up."

Jesus hung up the phone and Eli took down the list of things his mother needed.

Eli had to admit he was starting to like the few days a week he got to pick up David and Gloria at their after school program. It wasn't really putting him out to help Angelica with the kids. Entering the cafeteria, he saw David with his jet-black hair and deeply tanned skin. That kid had lived outside this summer. They had to drag him in the house if the sun was still out.

"David," he called, and David turned.

"Yes," David said as he made a fist, pumped his arm up and down, and ran to Eli who scooped him up like an expert.

"Where's your sister?"

"She's in the library."

Not surprising. "Let's go get her. We're going to Grandma's to drop off stuff on the way home."

David and Gloria burst through his mother's front door before he had a chance to open the trunk of his car. His mother met him at the door and helped with the bags.

"Jesus says you're seeing someone."

"Jesus has an avid imagination."

"Now don't lie to me, Elias. I can tell when you lie to me."

Eli turned to face his mother and caught her deep brown eyes with his. "Mama, I'm not dating anyone."

"You better not be just hooking up with her." She smacked him across the head with a dishtowel she carried in a secret place so it was always at the ready to assault her poor unsuspecting children. Growing up, he and his siblings swore she'd tied a lead weight in one for extra impact. "I know how you kids do it these days."

"I'm not discussing my sex life with you."

"So, you are defiling your body with some…some…"

Eli caught her shoulders to steady her before she went into a frenzy of Catholic prayers for her child's lost soul.

"Mama, I met my neighbor, who I assume is who Jesus is talking about. I still haven't met her husband, but her dad is really nice."

"Husband? Oh, *oso chiquito* I'm sorry I jumped to conclusions."

"Don't call me that," he whined. "It's bad enough everyone else calls me that."

His mother took his face in her hands and pulled him down to her.

"There is nothing wrong with being a teddy bear. Girls like the cuddly ones."

"And with that I'm going to take off. I need to feed the kids."

"I gave them each one cookie, nothing more. I know how Angelica is."

"Her you fear," he bemoaned.

"You really need to leave so soon?"

"No Mama," he said as he took a seat at the kitchen table. "I can stay a little bit longer."

* * * *

Almost a week had passed since Mary Beth had to deal with a man who wasn't a father. She had to admit she'd been hanging longer at the mailboxes and taking her time in the hall in hopes that new neighbor of hers would round a corner and bump into her again.

Through her door she heard a child speaking a mile a minute in Spanish. Grabbing her keys and laundry and rushing to her door, she opened to see Eli with a small boy on his hip and a little girl holding his free hand. The boy's arms were flailing as he told what must be an exciting tale.

"I'm sorry," Mary Beth said when her basket bumped the little girl's arm.

"It's okay," Eli replied, flashing an amazing smile at her.

Goose flesh tore across her body at the way his black eyes seemed to twinkle. Who knew a color so dark could exude peace and serenity?

"Gloria, David, this is my friend Mary Beth," Eli introduced the boy who was skinny as a rail and looked to be about Luke's age, maybe a little older. The girl had her hair pulled back into a thick ponytail and couldn't have been more than eight or nine. She had the most adorable chubby cheeks Mary Beth had ever seen.

"*Hola!*" They both said, then the girl pulled on Eli. "*Tío* come on."

"Just a minute," Eli said, pulling back on her arm. "I haven't seen my friend for a while."

"I got the light bulbs, thanks." Yeah that was the sexy purring every guy wanted.

"I'm glad. I didn't want to disturb you and your husband."

A strong rush of Catholic guilt tore through her. She had a child. Of course he thought she was married.

"I'm not married. Luke's dad…I have laundry."

She turned and headed toward the steps.

"I met your father and he said something about his son-in-law."

"I've never been married and I doubt my sisters have since they're still in school."

"Who's Maury?"

"Gabbie's dad. She's one of my business partners."

Eli placed David on the floor, gave his keys to Gloria, and said a few words in Spanish. Gloria looked at Eli, shook her head, and headed to the apartment.

"You're not with Luke's dad?" He smiled.

"No." Mary Beth bit on her lip and searched for the disappointment in Eli's eyes, but what she saw was something very different. "Is that a problem?"

"I think it solves a problem." Eli seemed to find an accent that caused heat to flare inside Mary Beth.

"What problem is that?"

"I can borrow more light bulbs."

Mary Beth raised her eyebrow at her neighbor.

"Maybe even some sugar, an egg or two. God knows I won't borrow your coffee."

"What's wrong with my coffee?" Mary Beth moved the laundry to her right hip and placed her free hand on her left.

"Nothing if you're just looking for bitter hot water." Eli stepped closer and Mary Beth felt her back against the wall. Her defiant hand dropped from her hip and she licked her lips. "Now, if you want something full-bodied, warm, and leaving you almost in tears when your cup is empty, let me know."

"Tears?" Mary Beth's lips trembled. Her chatty neighbor did know how to use his words at times.

"That is…until I refill it." Eli's finger traced along her jaw and the trembling engulfed her body. "Is that something you'd be interested in? Or do you only drink coffee for the caffeine kick and not for the experience?"

"You can have an experience with coffee?"

"You can have an experience with any of life's pleasures."

Mary Beth could feel her heart beating against her chest. Her head became light and she calculated exactly how many centimeters were between their lips.

"Coffee's a pleasure?" she asked in a strained whisper.

"Tsk, tsk, now I know why you allow that swill in your home. Polluting your body and never—"

"*Tío!*" Gloria yelled from the doorway. "I'll tell Mama what you're doing instead of feeding her starving children."

"Coming, princess," Eli replied with a much different tone then before, although his eyes stayed locked on Mary Beth's and his body didn't move.

Damn, between the heat of his body, the mischief in his eyes, and the sandalwood fragrance of his cologne, it took all of Mary Beth's strength to not melt against his body.

"I guess we'll have to have a coffee discussion later then," she said as she swallowed hard.

"Yes, and you need to get through some dirty laundry don't you?"

Laundry, a cold shower, and some other Hail Mary-worthy things.

Luckily she had her phone in her pocket, so as she loaded two washers she called Sarah, the next best thing.

"Hey."

"Hey yourself. What's up?"

"I just ran into my neighbor again."

"I hope he has bumpers."

"Not literally this time," Mary Beth groaned. "Is it possible to be turned on by a discussion of coffee?"

"This from the woman who gets wet when she's around Nate."

"I don't get wet around Nate."

"Oh, that's painful. Remind me to pick you up some lube next time I'm at the store."

"Not funny. You know what I mean."

"Okay, so old Juan Valdez turns you on, huh? Is it because he has a donkey and you've always been curious about spring break in Tijuana?"

"I was looking for a real discussion, you know, with my best friend about a man other than Nate."

"You're right. It was wrong of me to kid. So, does he have an accent, because let me tell you Selma Hayek could read me the phone book and I'd be drenched."

"Not all the time." Mary Beth thought about their latest interaction. "It's like he turns it on…"

"To turn you on? That's suspect. I mean we all do things, but if he becomes all native and can't speak without an accent only when your face is flushed and you're up against a wall—"

"How did you know about the wall?" Mary Beth balked.

"I have spy cameras on your door," Sarah scoffed. "Really? He had you pinned against a wall speaking in Spanish. Did he go all Shakira in *Hips Don't Lie*?"

"Yes, yes he did. He was wearing a dress and gyrating his hips with his abs flexed." Mary Beth shook her head. "Why did I call you?"

"Because Mandy will tell you to lock Luke in a closet with a juice box and some cookies and ride Mr. Chatty Cathy from here until Sunday. And Gabbie would demand he show you his resume before proceeding."

"She's lightened up," Mary Beth said. "She used to require a full credit check and FBI screening."

"I guess. So which is it? Interview or child neglect?"

"Neither. I want my sane friend to answer me."

"Oh, well, here's the deal. He's single and obviously interested so I'd say you're improving."

Mary Beth leaned against the table in the laundry room and clucked her tongue. "I think he has kids."

"Really?"

"Yes, two, Gloria and David. But he must be separated or something because the little girl threatened to tell her mother on him."

"Uh oh, you don't want any baby momma drama, just look at you and Nate."

"I don't cause any drama for Carrie."

"Besides sleeping with her husband," Sarah pointed out.

"Ouch."

"So you do need the lube?" she teased.

"Screw you."

"Oh, that'll be two Hail Marys for the language young lady."

"Yes and I'll abstain from liquor for a week."

Sarah paused for a moment then came back. "Truthfully, Mary Beth, any man that puts you and your feelings first is good in my book. Ever since junior high guys have been getting the best from you. They keep you on the line and before you know it...bam they're married to someone else."

"The last part only happened once."

"What about in your FACS class with Jimmy Bolton?"

"Family and consumer sciences?" Mary Beth asked with disdain. "The teacher assigned him to Heather, he didn't pick her."

"Um, not until two weeks later when he said he didn't like to go to dances and low and behold...bam, there he was, slow dancing in the middle of the gym because he didn't realize you had no problem rolling with your girls."

"Okay, you have a point. Eli doesn't have a ring on his finger and seems unattached."

"You've been checking out his finger?"

"Oh my God, I have. I might really like this guy."

"Just keep your cheatdar on high alert. You know how you like 'em attached and really unavailable. I gotta jet, I joined a bowling league, don't ask."

"Do I want to know the name of your team?"

"Chicks with Balls."

"No, I don't."

"It was either that or Girl on Girl Action, but that seemed a little too bold."

"Have fun Sarah, and thanks."

When Mary Beth returned to her apartment, Luke was finishing coloring in his homework. Damn, she needed to make a decision on the property. Luke's school was stifling him. He was too advanced to be coloring all the circles in the picture blue and all the squares red. Seriously, this was the state of public education. Thank God Gabbie and the girls actually had a lesson plan for the kids—even if it was loose, it was better than this crap.

"All done, Mama."

"Good job." She beamed and found a book for him to read to her.

* * * *

"Do you know what *tío* means?" Mary Beth asked Gabbie as they reviewed the survey questions she'd come up with.

"Theo?"

"No, *tío*. Gloria called Eli that. I think it means father or dad, but I'm not sure."

"Um, I was stuck in German with you, so no." Gabbie tapped her pen a few times absently on her pile of surveys. "But isn't it just poppy or something?"

"I don't know. I know it was a name she called him. Between that and his brother calling him *oso chiquito* I just feel lost around him and his family."

"How much of his family have you been around?"

"Not a lot and I mean I've only been around him in passing. It's just…"

"You feel like they're talking about you?"

"Sometimes."

"It amazes me how a woman who believes the world revolves around her, could raise a daughter that feels the same way. There's only one sun."

"What's that supposed to mean?"

"Your mother raised you to believe everyone was either talking about you or judging you. I'd be surprised if half the time people even noticed you."

"That's a crappy thing to say."

"You know that phrase about dancing like nobody's watching, you need to examine it. There are times I see you want to say something and then you bite your tongue. What's the worst that could happen? Someone takes it the wrong way? So what."

"And they think I'm a bitch or an idiot or..." Mary Beth could hear her mother's cutting words and felt the lump growing in her chest.

"Or what? A failure. Mary Beth I know what you fear and the worst thing is you'll never be a failure because you never try."

"You wouldn't even look at a guy for like five years after one bad boyfriend," she snapped.

"Keep deflecting, eventually it'll bounce back in your face."

Mary Beth turned back to her pile of surveys and ticked away responses, all the while cussing out her friend in her head. Gabbie didn't know how it felt to second, third, and fourth guess every comment you make. And when you finally feel comfortable with someone, you overstep and, as Sarah would say, bam, you're smacked in the face by it. They took it wrong or thought you were trying to hurt them when all you wanted was to have the fun good-natured conversation you'd seen them have with dozens of other people. Just not you. Never you. You were the antichrist people had to deal with.

Gabbie bounced her pen lazily between her fingers as she read a comment at the end of one of the surveys. She'd already moved past the fight they just had and all Mary Beth could do was rehash it and what she should have said and what she should have done.

"This is interesting," Gabbie said, passing the survey to Mary Beth. "This parent wants us to put together a presentation with veteran Montessorians and traditionalists to show the pros and cons."

"Great, now we need to jump through hoops." Mary Beth didn't have the time or patience for this.

"We need to educate the public if we want our dream to come true," Gabbie reasoned. "That's not asking a lot."

"Why do they have their kids here if they don't understand the process?"

"Because when it comes down to it we're a daycare center that just has a few added perks. Some places teach the kids sign language from six weeks old. Others offer special hours. Everyone has their gimmick."

"Oh, I didn't realize the Montessori method you've been treating as the next coming of Christ was a gimmick. I thought you believed in the principals and doctrine." Mary Beth didn't even understand why she was so irritated, but maybe it was because she just wanted one thing to go smoothly without having an issue.

"I do, but anything new is a gimmick. Got it? Even the Catholics had to plead their case when the Israelites were saying no, he's still dead."

"You had to go there didn't you?" Mary Beth asked knowing her friend was trying to get her back to center.

"Saw an opening and decided why not."

"How are we going to sell our snake oil?"

"I can get some people from the training center. I'm just not sure about the traditionalist. I doubt people will come and discuss why our method is better than theirs. But what you're missing is the bigger opportunity."

"That would be?"

"Reaching out to the community. We could stay open late one night and have the informal, yet formal discussion of our plans. Maybe show a few facilities we're thinking of purchasing and give a five and ten year forecast. You know that crap you go to school for."

"You mean the stuff I'm failing."

"And by failing you mean getting a B plus not an A?"

"Pretty much."

"Sweetie, the pressure you put on yourself is dangerous. No one is that perfect all the time."

"Speaking of being perfect, it's Friday and I have a little boy who doesn't have to ride the bus because his amazing mother can actually pick him up at school."

"Go have fun with the little monster."

A little while later, Mary Beth pulled up about a block away from Luke's elementary school. It'd be nice if she recognized any of the parents from orientation, but she felt like an outsider. Luke had talked about a few of his new friends and the possibility of going to play. Moms and dads congregated in bunches. Some held lattes or water bottles. She noticed a group of women in their thirties with exercise gear and perfect makeup. Although it appeared they might have been working out recently, they were vibrant and ready to take on the overactive child about to burst from the doors.

A few strollers held younger siblings and men tended to be on their phones with someone very important. Her search for a parent she could actually make a connection with came up empty and she stood in silence for the fourth week in a row at the edge of the sidewalk.

A loud bell sounded and teachers began filing out with kids. Luke told her he was excited she'd be picking him up every Friday. It's not that he didn't like the bus, but Mommy was always better. She could see his mop of blond hair and that he was in a very deep kindergarten conversation with a boy sporting a Mohawk.

"There she is," Luke called and took off at top speed.

Mary Beth knelt down and enveloped him in her arms. Even after a day of playing he still smelled of the no-tears shampoo and color on yourself soap. She looked into his beautiful, blue eyes that he got from his father and could see the pure, childish joy Mary Beth never wanted him to lose.

"Mama, I got a gold star on my shape worksheet. Can you meet Petey's mom? I wanna have him come over and play or go to his house."

A second later Mary Beth's arm was being pulled out of her socket as Luke suddenly had super human strength to drag her across the schoolyard.

"Petey...Petey...I gots my mom."

The little Mohawk wearing boy perked up and repeated the all out mom tug on one of the workout ladies.

31

"Hello," a nice lady with the same dark hair and olive skin coloring as Petey said as the two five-year-olds collided. "I'm Jessica, Pete's mom."

"I'm Mary Beth, Luke's mom."

"I've heard a lot about Luke. These two have been conspiring all week now."

Really? Luke hadn't mentioned anyone by name that she remembered.

"So where do you live?"

"In the apartments on Suburban."

Mary Beth had never felt ashamed of her apartment until Jessica gave a strange smile. Sure it wasn't a luxury condo or private home, but she could see Jessica's look of disappointment. A look that said why couldn't her son have picked a better off friend?

"Yeah, we have a pool on the inside so we can swim every day," Luke boasted. "But Mama only takes me on Mondays and Wednesdays."

"Why's that?" Jessica queried.

"There's usually no one there. We go for about a half hour or so. I just figured I can teach him how to swim, but we didn't want to disturb others with the flopping."

"Yeah, Mama's taught me to pizza slice."

"I don't know that method. It sounds like fun. Let me get your number, Mary Beth, and we'll see about getting the boys together one afternoon."

"Friday's are the only afternoons I have off."

"I don't work so he could come to our house. We're over in the Beaver Creek neighborhood a little behind those apartments."

They exchanged numbers. Mary Beth felt compelled to explain why this would probably never work.

"His dad is one of those last minute dads. I'll try to plan, but I might have to cancel if his dad decides he wants him for the afternoon."

"You don't have a custody agreement?" she asked with a crooked face that made the acid in Mary Beth's nervous stomach creep up.

"We get along and…"

"It's not about getting along, it's about giving Luke structure." Jessica dropped the concerned face and her dark ponytail bounced from side to side as she shook her head. "You know what, I'm putting on my social worker hat and I'll stop. Ten years of working in the field it's sometimes hard to shut my mouth. How about next Tuesday you can send a note to school and if his dad doesn't show up Luke can come play at our house."

"Sounds good, I work until six if it's okay to pick him up that late. If not..."

"It'll be fine," she assured and placed her hand on Mary Beth's forearm.

"Bye Jess," a few of the ladies called, and she waved.

"Again, it's not my place, but at this age Luke really needs stability. You should consider a schedule with his dad."

As Jessica walked away Mary Beth went over the first few weeks of school in her mind. Luckily she'd been able to avoid Nate, but that wasn't good for Luke who was starting to miss his dad. He'd only spent two afternoons with him since the last time they were together intimately and although it was good for her to have the break from Nate, Luke was another story. She just hated having to call and ask him to spend time with his own son.

As she loaded Luke in her minivan she smiled at her boy. He really did roll with the punches. The few times Mary Beth's dad had been gone for more than a day she felt as if a part of her was gone, but not Luke. He knew his dad just wasn't going to be there.

"What do you say, Lukey, a movie and some chicken tonight?"

* * * *

A flash of red passed by Eli's office as he was hit with the three-thirties. If only his niece and nephew hadn't been over on Tuesday, he'd have had Mary Beth right then and there. He could feel the electricity between the two of them. What a satisfying rush. To wake up, Eli opted for fresh air instead of better living through chemistry.

As the glass doors parted he was hit with the nice cool fall air and saw the flash again. Only this time, the flash had legs that went on forever. Mary Beth sat sideways in her older model maroon minivan with its door open and her feet resting on the running board. Her face was scrunched in frustration.

"You could have just come in and said hi," he started, and her face softened a little. "Whatcha doing out here?"

"Waiting on Maury."

"Hey, Eli," Luke called from his booster seat in the back. "Mama's letting me eat in the car." He waved a half-eaten leg of fried chicken.

"Do I get a piece?" he teased.

"I dunno, ask Mama?"

"You really want a piece?"

"Are we still talking about chicken?" Eli asked with a raised eyebrow.

"At the moment." Mary Beth's lips twitched into a small smile.

"Maybe later. Is something wrong with your van?"

"Only everything. I keep waiting for a push, pull or drag sale, but I wouldn't be able to get a new car anyway."

"You'd be surprised. The rates are dropping. People are getting some great deals. Maury said you own your own business, is it profitable?"

"Am I applying for a loan right now?"

"That's my job. I process the loans for this branch."

"Seriously?"

"Yep, car, personal, and even a few home and business ones occasionally. I have tomorrow off. We could put through a loan app and I could take you car shopping tomorrow. If you're free."

"I don't like taking out loans."

"Nope, she doesn't," Maury said as he approached. "She just likes bothering me a dozen times a week to keep this scrap heap together."

"Maury!" Luke squealed and hopped out of his seat.

"Lukey, give me a hug or I'm gonna make your mama pay me in chicken to fix this car." Luke gave Maury a bear hug. "Special day, eating chicken in the car."

"Yep. I ate two legs."

"Then how are you gonna walk home?" Maury teased.

"Not *my* legs, silly."

"That's good to know. Can you pop the hood for me?"

Luke obliged, having become an expert at pulling the release, and Maury tinkered with a few things until the van roared to life.

"I volunteer Maury's daycare services if you go with him tomorrow and get a new car." Maury hitched his thumb toward Eli.

Eli grinned. "There are worse things than a small car note."

"Yeah, like putting me in an early grave fearing you'll break down on the highway." Maury put his tools away. "Go with him. The scrap value alone will get you five hundred."

"It'd take me ten minutes to process your application."

"Will this hunk of junk start up again in fifteen minutes?"

"It's possible. How about Luke and I hit the deli while you run the numbers? Just in case."

Mary Beth shrugged and locked her van.

Eli walked beside her and made sure to brush the back of his hand against hers. She turned and smiled, but kept walking silently.

In his office Eli woke his computer and pulled up a blank application.

"Mary Beth what?"

"What?"

"Your last name, you still haven't told me."

"Wallace."

He typed away asking questions when necessary and as he ran her credit he leaned back in his chair.

"Why is eating in your van so special?"

"When Luke was about two I learned why my mother never let us eat in the car."

"Couldn't you just teach him to not spill?"

"A better mother probably could. But an exhausted mother in the first full year running her own business...let's just say if it wasn't for my friends he'd probably still be in diapers."

"I doubt that, I've seen you with him. There's love, anything else is just a bonus."

Mary Beth shifted in her chair as the cutest flash of red Eli had ever seen exploded across her cheeks.

"Why is that embarrassing?"

"It's not, I just...I'm not a good mom, trust me. Sometimes I wonder..." her voice trailed off and she pulled into herself. "Can I get a car or not?"

"What kind of car are you interested in?" Eli asked.

"A reliable one."

"Come on, everyone has their dream car," he reasoned.

"I'm a mom, I care about gas mileage and safety."

"And you drive that piece of crap van?"

"That how you talk to all your customers?"

"Only the ones I'm trying to keep safe." The timber in his voice betrayed him almost as much as his words. Damned if he wasn't falling hard and quick for this woman.

"You want to keep me safe?"

"That scare you?"

His computer beeped—Mary Beth looked through the glass to the check-out lines to avoid his question.

"What's the verdict?"

"I'll need the real documentation to put this deal through, but I can hold it for twenty-four hours at a three point seven interest rate up to eighteen thousand dollars."

"Seriously?"

"With your credit and income, yes. Are you saving for a home?"

"No, I could never afford that."

"Not a mansion, but you're in amazing shape, considering."

"Considering what?"

"Single mom. Most are really struggling. How about we hit highway sixty-one around ten and test drive some cars and afterward we can have dinner."

"That's a lot of test driving."

"You'd be surprised how long the paperwork takes. Is it a date?"

"A date? That ups it quite a bit."

"Why?"

"I haven't been on a date for a while."

"Define awhile."

"Let's see, Luke's five, add about seven months and...yeah, never really. His dad and I would hang out in groups, not really date. Before him it was basically the same thing."

"And I thought it took a village to raise a child, not conceive it."

"Ha, ha you're so funny."

"So, you, me and an adult beverage or two?" Eli asked with a smirk and hope.

"After I get a new car, we'll see."

* * * *

On the way home Luke chatted away about a myriad of things, but all Mary Beth could focus on was Eli. Had he really asked her out on a date? What does one do on a date? More importantly what does one wear? She'd been sitting in her van for a while parked before Luke finally groaned and broke her focus.

"Mama, it's Friday, I get cartoons for an hour. Let's go."

"You're right, sorry, you know how Mama wanders sometimes."

With Luke fed and distracted, Mary Beth picked through her closet. When did she become such a mom? Her shirts were mostly boat or square necked, except the virginity-protecting turtle necks that had failed miserably in high school. Buried deep she did find a few skirts that all seemed too young for her now. Goodwill was calling her closet, that was for sure.

There was one skirt left that wasn't young looking.

"Mary Beth, I can't believe you put that on to go to church. You look like a gypsy."

Guess her mother hadn't seen what a modern day gypsy wore. The echoes of admonishment made Mary Beth second-guess the skirt. It was a pale turquoise with little flowers cut on the top layer of cotton. With a sewn in lining, there was no skin to show, especially since the skirt almost came to her ankles. What had been so wrong with it?

"It's beautiful," Eli's deep voice made her turn quickly. "I hope you wear it tomorrow."

"Why are you in my bedroom?"

"Luke let me in."

"Lucas Nathan Wallace." Mary Beth stormed from her room, leaving the skirt behind. "What have I told you about answering the door? And you let someone in?"

"It's just Eli," he replied, not turning his head from the latest *Adventures of Gumball.*

37

"That's not the point. You can't even see out into the hallway to know it was him."

"He said it was Eli," Luke reasoned. "Mama, I'm big enough to know when it's Eli or not?"

"No, you're not. Next time tell him to wait and come get me."

"Why?"

"Your mom's right," Eli interjected. "I wouldn't have minded standing in the hall for a few minutes waiting on you to get her."

"Don't do it again or no cartoons at all next week." An extreme punishment from Mary Beth, but she needed to get her point across.

"Okay, Mama."

Finally turning to Eli, Mary Beth let out an exasperated breath. "Why are you here?"

"I got locked out and I was hoping you knew what Maury does to pop the lock."

"I don't, but are your windows open by chance?"

"Yes."

"Those I can pop. One of the blessings of being on the lower level. Luke, I'm going outside for a minute to help Eli. Do *not* answer the door for anyone, you hear me?"

"You might want to augment that statement," Eli suggested.

"Why?"

"Gloria and David are in my apartment, and they won't open the door for me."

"You're breaking into your apartment, because your kids won't open the door?"

Eli shrugged and Mary Beth grabbed her own keys off the counter.

"No one, Lucas."

"Yes, Mama," he called back.

"And a bath as soon as the cartoon is over."

"Awe, man."

"No aweing me, mister."

When they were outside Mary Beth walked to where Eli's apartment was.

"Again, why won't the kids open the door for you?"

"Their mom said not to open the door to anyone...ever."

38

"Oh, so some kids do listen to their mothers."

"Only every other thing. So tell Luke a few more random rules then slip that one in again."

Mary Beth tried not to smile too much at him.

"All right, this will be easier with you. Give me a boost."

Eli placed one knee on the ground and kept the other one up and she stepped on his thigh. When she looked in the apartment David and Gloria screamed bloody murder as Mary Beth raised her eyebrow to them.

"Now, it'll take me less than two minutes to get this screen open and climb in to let your *tío* in. You've got a choice to make. Open the door for him or have one very upset redheaded mama coming in."

Gloria took off to the door and unlocked it for Eli. Jumping down, Mary Beth smiled at Eli.

"Your door's open."

"Was that your plan the whole time?"

"No, I can break in, but it's easier boosting a five-year-old in then climbing in myself."

"I'll have to remember to lock my windows. I'd hate to have an angry redheaded mama coming through my window." Eli leaned in close and Mary Beth felt her heart flutter. "Then again…"

His hand cradled her head as his thumb stroked her bottom lip. His eyes told his intentions.

"Mary Beth, can I kiss you?"

Mary Beth's lips throbbed as she breathed in the fresh smell of his cologne. Yes. Yes. Yes. Only the words didn't come out. Instead she froze as she looked in his eyes. Why couldn't she kiss this man? He was attractive, sweet, and kind. She didn't have a boyfriend. Just a damn baby daddy—who wasn't even that.

"Have you ever really lost control?"

"What do you mean?" she asked, breathlessly.

"I can see you holding back, but I can't tell why yet. There is fire behind your eyes…" Eli licked his lips and Mary Beth whimpered. "Maybe after dinner tomorrow." Eli headed inside.

"Shit," Mary Beth cursed under her breath. "I hate you, Nate. So damn much."

Walking back into her apartment, Luke had already turned off the cartoons and was pulling out bath toys. His mop of blond hair reminded her of Nate when they were in high school, back when pro scouts were looking at him and when he talked about forever.

"We doing bubbles tonight?" she asked as she wiped a tear of frustration from her cheek before she started the water.

With Luke in bed, Mary Beth finally remembered her mail. After retrieving it, she was about to go into her apartment when she saw Eli hugging a woman. She had long, thick, black hair pulled up in a ponytail. She had the same complexion as Eli and wore a set of maroon scrubs. Eli pulled back and kissed her forehead, then nose and both cheeks.

He was still together with his children's mother. The cheating bastard was trying to kiss her just a few hours ago! Mary Beth didn't slam the door when she entered her apartment. She was eerily calm about the whole situation.

Chapter Four

If you fall, I'll be there.

—The Floor

Mary Beth woke with a stiff back after a knock on her door brought her back into the here and now. Sunlight shone through the window, blinding her return to the land of the living. Had she shut down that much? Another knock had her stiffly getting up to open the door.

"Hey, Mary Beth," Maury said. As he walked in his voice trailed. "You okay?"

"Fine, I don't need Maury's babysitting services. I'm not getting a new car today."

"Where's Luke?"

"I just got up." She walked toward Luke's room and saw it was nine-thirty. He had to be up by now.

"That's evident."

Luke was sitting on his floor, eating a bowl of cereal, and playing racecars.

"You got your own cereal?" Mary Beth wiggled her toes and finally registered the wetness from what she could only assume was spilled milk.

"Yeah, you didn't want to."

"Did I say that?"

"You didn't say nothing. That's when I gots my own bowl."

"Mary Beth." Maury placed his hand on her shoulder. "Have you been drinking?"

"No. I fell asleep by the door, that's all."

41

"You do that often enough that Lukey knows to get his own bowl of cereal."

"No, damn it, Maury…"

"Mama." Luke's head popped up. "You said a swear."

"I'm sorry. Mama's just got a headache."

"Do I need to go to Auntie Sarah's again?"

"Luke." Her stomach tightened as her face flushed red.

When the next knock echoed through the apartment Mary Beth felt her spine tingle with anger. It could only be one person. The latest man wanting her to be the other damn woman. Not. This. Time.

"What?" she snarled as she yanked the door open.

Eli looked over his shoulder sure her rage was for a monster behind him.

"Did I get the wrong day?"

"You got the wrong woman. Go back to your wife."

Mary Beth slammed the door, satisfied in her decision. She'd finally drawn a line in the sand. If only she could do that with Nate.

"But I'm not married," Eli said through the door. "I've never even been engaged."

"Then go back to your baby mama. Either way I saw you last night."

Mary Beth stood with her back to the door and her arms crossed. Maury stood at the edge of the kitchen with a very confused look on his face.

"I'm taking myself back," she explained to Maury. "I'm giving up Nate, and I'm not about to start another relationship the same way."

"I'm not arguing, but he doesn't seem the type."

"You didn't see him…" Mary Beth's voice rose. "Making out with her in the hallway last night."

"If you think that was making out you need to be kissed a hell of lot better than you have been," Eli said through the door. "Can you please open the door?"

Maury pushed past Mary Beth and opened the door.

"So you're saying you were kissing a girl last night."

"It wasn't a girl. It was my sister."

Eli looked over Maury's shoulder to Mary Beth whose face burned even brighter now.

"Again, woman, you need to be kissed by someone with technique. That was the sign of the cross that our grandmother does as a blessing to us kids."

Forehead, nose, cheek, cheek...no lips.

"Your sister? I'm supposed to believe you?"

"She's cooking my niece and nephew breakfast."

"David and Gloria aren't your kids?"

"Nope, I have no kids." He then winked at Maury. "That I know of...you feel me...no... Right."

"Then why do they call you *tío*?"

"Because it means uncle in Spanish, what did you think it meant?"

"Well—really? Uncle?"

"We tend to go with Dad and Mama. The real question is why are you so mad?"

"I'm not mad."

Maury coughed bullshit and left to get Luke out of his pajamas.

"So, no skirt."

"You don't think I'm a psycho?"

"I'm more then sure you are, but I was raised with women who threw heavy objects when pissed and could take your eye out with a dish towel. You're a lightweight. Speaking of which, you want to meet my sister Angelica?"

"Why do you watch her kids?"

"Um...she's my sister...and her husband's in Afghanistan. She normally works three to three at a hospital. It's hard getting afternoon and night baby sitters. Last night she got a phone call from her husband and they let her go early because she couldn't stop crying."

"He's not hurt is he?"

"He got stop-lossed so he's got another tour to do. He was supposed to be retiring in a month."

"That's horrible."

"That's why she crashed on my couch. She didn't want to go home with the kids alone." Eli slapped his hands together and smiled. "Skirt, maybe a shower and we're off to the car lot?"

* * * *

"I'm going to drive you crazy if you take me to the car lot. I'm cheap and whiny and hate change."

"Well, I look at it this way. I just have to get you to a car lot and your minivan will die again. Maury already planned on ignoring all your calls today, so you'll be stuck."

Maury walked out with Luke who had his little backpack on and was ready to head out.

"Mandy's going to pick Luke up and bring him home later. I've got a date with my lady."

"You two are in cahoots aren't you?" Mary Beth pointed to Eli and Maury.

"You think it's just two of us," Maury scoffed as he and Luke passed. "We got a good half dozen signed up to support this one."

"You're planning something, aren't you?" Mary Beth suspiciously eyed Eli as Luke gave her a goodbye kiss on the cheek before shutting the door.

"Me? Plan something? I'm a guy, we'd never look more than three minutes ahead."

"Then why are you grinning?" Mary Beth accused.

"Cuz in three minutes, the shampoo will be sliding down your wet backside."

Mary Beth stepped back in utter disbelief, so Eli made his move and turned her so she was pinned against the wall.

"Or…" he began as he leaned in and brushed her neck with his nose to smell her soft scent. Damn her skin was so soft. "Will you have one of those poufy things rubbing between your breasts?"

"I have…have…no…idea…"

"Oh please, we both have more than one idea when it comes to what you should be doing in the shower. If you want, I'd be more than happy to come in and tell you how you should wash your delicate skin."

"I'm more than capable of washing myself. Have been for years."

Eli stepped back and held up three fingers. "Let me guess, since you were this many?"

Mary Beth clutched his hand and bent his ring finger down gently. Eli felt a rush headed straight to his groin.

"This many," she practically purred.

"I like early achievers. They don't mind stepping up the pace."

He leaned and kept his eyes locked on hers. If she closed hers it was on. He was going to get the kiss he'd been aching three weeks for. Instead she licked her top lip and he had to steel himself to keep his distance.

"Ducha?" he whispered, unsure if he'd be able to be this close for much longer without turning this encounter into a bad telenovela.

"That is?"

"Shower, you know, that thing you need to…" He sighed and tried to pull himself from her draw.

"Alone," she said and her lips brushed against his. As she pulled away her face was flushed again, and he swore he heard *this time* as she closed the door and turned on the spray.

"Oh my God, Eli, what the hell are you doing?" he scolded himself and looked at his crotch. "How the hell am I going to get rid of this in the next ten minutes?"

With his manhood strong and throbbing, Eli tried envisioning dead puppies and financial reports. Anything to get rid of the feeling of Mary Beth's lips softly brushing against his.

It took a half hour for Mary Beth to get out of the shower and dressed. She acted rushed the whole time. He thought his sister and cousins were bad. The worst part is she seemed to have reverted back to all-business-no-chance-of-anything-Mary Beth.

As they drove along the two miles worth of car dealers on highway sixty-one, Mary Beth attempted the prayer of the owners with bad vehicles. First it was the encouraging, "Yeah girl, I knew you were going to be good to me." Followed by the threatening, "I swear to God if you die at the stoplight I'll send you to the crusher." And finally the lying pleader… "Girl, just make it to the lot. I'm not selling you, sweetheart, I'm taking Eli car shopping."

They pulled into a lot where Mary Beth saw forty-two MPG scrawled on a sign in the windshield of a smaller sedan.

"I could down grade in size. I got this more for hauling crap and it was cheap."

"Why did it take you so long in the shower?"

"Um…I didn't take that long."

"It took you five minutes to get dressed and twenty-five minutes to shower. Any woman that can look as amazing as you do right now in five minutes takes shorter showers."

"Is there a Harvard study on this or are you going on pure experience?"

"You did something in the shower, didn't you?"

"I have no idea what you're talking about." Her face flashed bright red.

"That is so not fair. I had to get over my want to take you against the wall, and you just used a shower head."

"First, the shower head is not removable—"

"So you thought about it."

"I didn't! Why do...ugh."

When the green flecks in her eyes began to sparkle, Eli knew he'd been forgiven.

"Admit it, you can't resist me."

"Is that a challenge?"

"Depends. What do I get when you pin me against the wall and demand I take you like the animal I am?"

Mary Beth burst in a fit of laughter. "That could never happen."

"What's so funny?"

"The idea of me overpowering you."

Eli leaned across the center console and felt the heat coming off Mary Beth.

"You don't think your uncontrollable lust for me could give you superhuman strength?"

"Uncontrollable? I think I've been more than under control with you."

"That's why you took so long in the shower. How cold was the water?"

Mary Beth's bottom lip trembled and when she tried to look away Eli caught her chin and turned it toward him.

"Face me and say it."

"Not cold enough." She was practically breathless.

"You can't lie when you look at me, can you?"

She chose silence over telling him the truth.

Holding firm to her chin Eli went for broke. "Do you want to kiss me?"

"Yes."

"Why don't you?"

"It's a long story."

"Same reason you've never been on a date? Because you're stuck in high school?"

"It's not like that."

"Fine, I'll stop asking. You're the one losing out anyway." Eli dropped his hand from her chin and got out of the van.

"Seriously," Mary Beth growled as she slammed her car door and came to confront him. "I'm losing out? You're the one losing out. I kiss you and you'd be on your knees, buddy. How could I possibly lose out from not—"

No more being a gentleman and asking a woman who didn't know what she wanted if she wanted him.

He pressed her against the passenger door and claimed her mouth. As his tongue swept through her trembling lips his hand glided over her short hair. Damn this woman for cutting it short. Even though it framed her face beautifully, he wanted to get lost in a tangled mess of red hair. Mary Beth didn't fight him. In fact, soon she was running her finger through his hair, clutching his shoulders, and then hitching her right leg around him.

Her tongue darted into his mouth. He adjusted his hips and thrust them against her as his left hand found her ankle and worked its way under her skirt. Heat seared his lips from her taste and passion. There was a fire inside his little redheaded neighbor that needed to be tapped, and quickly.

"Excuse me," a man's voice said. "If you'd like one last roll in the backseat we could drive her around back."

"I'm sorry," Eli said as he pulled his head back and Mary Beth turned hers away from the salesman. "A red head and Latino, when sparks fly we tend to stoke them instead of put them out."

Eli's left hand had made its way to Mary Beth's bare thigh. Even with the salesman watching he couldn't help pressing his hard length against her stomach. Mary Beth turned, wide-eyed, and then looked down. Reaching with his free right hand, Eli got down to the business that sadly was at hand.

"I'm Eli, this is my friend Mary Beth. She's looking for a new car."

The salesman took his hand and shook.

"Can you two unhook and we'll see what we can get her into?"

"I can't stay here now," Mary Beth whispered to Eli.

"Yes you can, we've already met…what's your name?"

"Bill."

"Bill, and I have a feeling he'll be more than happy to help us."

Bill turned to walk toward the salesroom and Eli finally let go of Mary Beth's thigh so she could drop her foot to the ground.

"I can't believe that just happened," she said as she covered her face with her hand. "I've never… Oh my God."

"I'm just mad I didn't get to find out what you were or weren't wearing under that skirt of yours."

Bill turned back to them and Eli pushed off the car and pulled Mary Beth with him. To Eli's relief, she strategically placed herself in front of him just enough to hide the erection he feared may never be relieved, especially with Mary Beth's ass brushing against it. With his hands on her hips he moved himself back just enough so there wasn't direct contact.

"Darn, I was enjoying that," she growled.

"Woman, you really don't want to go in that showroom do you?"

"Oh, but I do, I'm going to tease your ass for at least three test drives."

* * * *

"So, how were you raised?" Eli asked as they waited for their appetizer.

Mary Beth had enjoyed her day toying with Eli and his probably very sore by now manhood. Even now she was tempted to let her foot travel further up his leg under the table. He had a very talented tongue and Mary Beth was more than a little inclined to see his full skill set.

Damn he was cute and a tease that wasn't ashamed to stroke her thigh in public. He wasn't worried what anyone thought and he seemed to have a possessive need to touch her—especially around other men.

"Irish Catholic, and you?"

"Same, minus the Irish."

"A hundred percent of the guilt."

"Not really. I'd go to confession and my mother would have loved if at least one of us would have donned the cloth, but she was never a 'damn your soul to Hell' kind of mother."

"And your father?"

"Went to make my mother happy. You still go every Sunday?"

"Um, I'm not welcome at my parish. I keep my own council now."

"You could check out mine. Half the guilt and better pastries."

"We'll see."

"Maury's your friend's dad, so why are you two so close?"

"We weren't until I got pregnant. I was Daddy's girl all my life until I really needed him. Gabbie's always been less dependent on her dad... Don't get me wrong, they get along great and have this secret language and all. Maury stepped up to fill a very large hole in my life. You know until you asked I never noticed how much I do depend on him. There was almost a seamless transition between my dad and him. In a way I'm lucky because I never really felt alone."

Mary Beth set down her cosmo and shook her head. With a long sip of her water she sobered herself.

"I'm so sorry, that was over sharing in its purest form."

"I liked it. I know sometimes it's hard to get a word in edgewise with me. When did your father pass away?"

"My father's alive," Mary Beth said with a hard gulp.

"Then why did Maury step in?"

"Irish Catholic. I didn't get married and I didn't go away to a special home for unwed mothers."

"It's not the sixties."

"Tell my mother. She didn't want my younger siblings to think what I did was acceptable behavior."

"When was the last time you saw them?"

"They live in the area so I've seen them a few times, but they turn and go the other way as if I were a stranger."

Eli was speechless for the first time ever.

"I have my best friends and they've always been sisters to me. I mean..."

Across the room Mary Beth saw her father sitting in a back booth. She knew it was him, but the woman with him was not her mother. Her mother's hair matched her own, only it was long and usually controlled by a bun. This woman's hair was a deep, chestnut brown and it luxuriously flowed past her shoulders. If Mary Beth didn't know better she'd have thought... The woman turned to the waiter and the side of her face was unmistakable.

"Mary Beth? You okay?"

"My father's over there." Her voice, barely above a whisper.

"Over where?" Eli turned and scanned the restaurant.

"He's the one feeding his cheesecake to Ariel, Mandy's mom."

"Who's Mandy?"

"You'll meet her tonight. She's picking up Luke from Maury's and watching him for me." Mary Beth could not pull her eyes from the scandal of all scandals happening before her. Her father took Ariel's hand in his. "Excuse me."

Making a beeline for her father, Mary Beth blocked out the noise around her. All she could see was the man she'd always counted on, cheating on her mother.

"How long?" she snapped when she got to the table, pulling the two would be lovers from their moment. "How long have you two been together? You can't tell me this is just some parent planning meeting for a fundraiser."

"Mary Beth...it's not what it seems," Ariel started to say, but Mary Beth held up her hand to stop her.

"You kick me out of my family for getting pregnant and you're having an affair." Her father stared at her, but didn't respond. "Talk to me. I'm your goddamn daughter and I deserve an explanation."

"Are you?"

The condemnation in his voice was like a roundhouse kick to her chest.

"Ma'am, I'm going to have to ask you to return to your table," a man said as he placed his hands on her shoulders.

"Get your hands off her," Eli warned.

"Sir, she's causing a scene."

"You want a bigger one," he growled. "She'll sit down in a minute, until then everyone here gets dinner and a show. You'll be able to charge double."

"Kevin, she deserves to know," Ariel said and broke the tension. "This has gone on long enough."

"How long?"

"Before you were born," Ariel confessed.

And now it was a line drive to her chest.

"How?"

"Can I at least ask you to join them?" the annoyed manager begged.

"Bring her a chair. I'm pretty sure she doesn't want to sit next to either of them," Eli ordered, and then slid in next to Ariel.

Finally sitting Mary Beth bounced between the two adulterers.

"But you've never dated anyone." She glared at Ariel. "I thought Mandy was living in a fantasy world. I mean her father abandons you, of course you'll eventually fall for someone, but—"

The realization of the previous admission sent the spreadsheets of information in her head into sum mode.

"Before I was born. How long before I was born?"

"About seven months." Her father confessed.

Ariel's head bowed in shame.

"Mandy's only three months younger than me."

"Ariel worked in my office. I panicked when your mother said she was pregnant. Ariel was there."

"When a woman gets pregnant you get a drink and figure out how to pay for the hospital bill. You don't go fuck another woman." Mary Beth's fist smashed into the tabletop, bouncing wine glasses and silverware.

"Language. I'm still your father."

"You ceased being my father when you kicked me out for making a mistake. That's why my mother always hated you and Mandy. Why she tried to get me to hate her. Mandy's my..."

Vomit rose in Mary Beth's throat as she thought of one of her best friends. The one with the dark hair and hazel eyes. Their father's eyes only Mandy's had dark brown specks like her mother's.

"Why did you allow us to be friends?"

"We couldn't stop it," Ariel explained. "By the end of the first practice you guys had already planned sleepovers for the rest of the summer. The four of you were inseparable and by the time your mother came to practice and saw your new best friend was my daughter it was too late."

"That's why you doted on her when she came over. You said it was because she didn't have a dad. So you two kept going all these years. Why did you stay with mom?"

"It's complicated."

"No, it's not. You could have left years ago."

"There was always a baby on the way and then we fell into an acceptable routine." Her father's explanation was as weak as Nate's always were.

"I guess that Irish Catholic guilt only works on the women in your family." Eli nervously laughed to break the tension, and then shrugged his shoulders in apology.

"Your mother has darkened in the last few years—"

"Darkened? As in stopped allowing you to have a mistress and her?"

"…And Ariel and I are moving forward with our life together."

"What the hell does that mean?"

"We're getting married." Ariel reached across the table to hold Mary Beth's father's hands.

"Divorce? You're divorcing Mom? She's going to lose it."

"She'll be fine. It's not like she didn't know about Ariel."

"Why now? Mandy and I are grown. What purpose does it serve?"

"Jillian's in high school now. I've raised her the best I could and the rest of you are living your lives. There really isn't a reason to be there."

"Except to be with the woman you swore to love until the day you die. Yeah, I see nothing."

Mary Beth pushed up from the table. Her chair shot across the floor as she headed for the door. Instead of having the pleasure of shoving it open, Eli was there opening it for her, and the second they were outside of the restaurant he pulled her into his arms.

Mary Beth's life was collapsing around her, and instead of telling her he had somewhere to be, Eli was there. Holding her up. Taking care of her.

"I'm sorry," she said as she pulled away from him and headed to her new car. "I have a temper sometimes."

"No, you don't say. I prefer when it's against me, but I'll be here for you when it's others."

"It's just...you don't..."

"You don't need to explain."

"I don't want to be her."

"Ariel?"

"No, well yes, but not her or my mother. They're both so..."

Mary Beth shook and Eli took the keys to her car away.

"I'll drive so I don't have to learn how well your car corners at ninety," he ordered and ushered her to the passenger door. "You vent. We don't want Luke seeing you like this."

As they drove back to the apartment building Mary Beth cursed the day she was born as well as a few dozen other things. Unlike her normal outbursts, that she'd be able to reign in after a few minutes, this time she got it all out. She wasn't re-corking the bottle while the champagne overflowed.

When they pulled into a parking space she felt a weight release from her chest. The headache so constant she'd forgotten what it was like to live without at least some dull ache behind her forehead was gone. She was lightheaded and it wasn't from the few sips of her drink. Eli was still there.

"Better?" Eli's voice was calm and velvety.

"The world's a little wonky right now." Mary Beth swallowed the acid burning its way up her throat.

"Physically?"

"Yes."

"That happens when you blow a gasket. I know the cure-all though."

"And that would be?"

Eli pointed forward and Mary Beth noticed they were parked in front of a *Dairy Queen.*

53

"What's your poison? And don't worry they've got chairs outside so we won't be eating in your car."

"I think I deserve a banana split."

"Before dinner? I guess so."

Eli got out and led her to a red, chicken wire picnic table. When he returned, he had a hamburger basket and a banana split.

"I don't know about you, but I'm hungry. This crazy lady dragged me to a half dozen dealerships looking at car after car. None of which had a decent backseat in my humble opinion. Then you know what she did?"

"What?" Mary Beth smiled.

"Went back to the first dealer and bought the first car she saw."

"I liked Bill and I'm pretty sure we didn't go to a half dozen." Mary Beth scooped some of the pineapple part of her split, then let the cold sweetness melt in her mouth.

"You're right, it might have been two dozen."

She slapped at Eli and scooped some chocolate. Yeah, this was what she needed. The buzzing in her head was coming down as she cut a piece of banana off.

"What was wrong with the backseats?"

"She's this sexy ass lady with legs from here to Hinckley. Which means even wrapped around my waist we couldn't fit back there."

"Only to Hinckley?" Mary Beth asked and extended her legs by pointing her toes.

Eli took a long look as if he was really gauging the length. When he put his hand on her thigh and began scrunching the fabric so it slowly showed skin he breathed in, but not out.

Mary Beth couldn't understand how a simple thing could cause her skin to rise and the swooning in her head came back, but in a much different way. As her knee became exposed Eli finally breathed out.

"Canada, definitely. Her legs go all the way to Canada."

"Thank you for this," she said as she scooped strawberry covered ice cream.

"It's self-preservation. I really am hungry." He let her skirt go and the soft fabric caressed her leg as it fell to her ankle again. "And I do like you. I don't know what I would have done if I'd seen what you did today."

"Now I have to go home and tell my best friend she's my sister. Her lousy, no good, dead beat dad is mine."

"I'll stay if you want me to."

"No, I think my ego's had enough embarrassment for one day."

"I told you they'd catch us, but you had to force yourself on me at the car dealership."

"Other way around."

"No, I was completely under your spell." Eli cupped her cheek—Mary Beth closed her eyes and nuzzled against his palm. "I had no control over my actions. Like right now."

With a gentle touch Eli once again kissed her. This time without the passion from earlier in the day—the passion had been replaced with something Mary Beth had never truly experienced, but she recognized it instantly. Love.

Chapter Five

"A friend is someone who knows all about you and still loves you."
—Elbert Hubbard

"Mandy?" Mary Beth called as she entered her apartment.

"Oh my God," Mandy said as she came out of the bathroom with her hand on her stomach. "I think I just lost five pounds. Let the vent work in there for a few—"

Mandy finally noticed Mary Beth wasn't alone as her lip curled at Eli.

"Well, hello. Excuse me, I didn't know my girl had a guest."

"Mandy, this is my neighbor Eli," Mary Beth said as she laid her keys on the counter and steadied herself.

"Well, won't you be my neighbor," Mandy practically growled.

"Ignore her," Mary Beth said aghast. "Most people don't listen to a word she says."

"At least not since I stopped talking while giving blow jobs. Everyone used to say I mumble but now—"

"Now I wonder why I thought you could watch my son."

"Technically, Maury thought I was mature enough to watch Luke, the damn fool."

"Right." Mary Beth turned to Eli. "I need to do this alone. Thank you for today."

"See you tomorrow."

"I look forward to it." With Eli safely outside Mary Beth shoved Mandy. "What the hell was that?"

"A little harmless flirting. He's got the biggest puppy dog eyes."

"And?" Mary Beth practically growled.

"And what?" Mandy placed her hands on her hips. "You're sleeping with Carrie's husband aren't you?"

"Not funny."

"You like him?" Mandy's eyebrows rose in shock.

"I don't know. Yes. No. Well…either way."

"You've been Nate's girl since before he asked you out."

"I have not," Mary Beth said, defiantly.

"I'm sorry." Mandy cocked her head to the side and twirled her index finger. "Who else have you slept with?"

"Bitch."

"Hester."

"Hester?"

"Do I need a red A for your chest?"

"Pot."

"Kettle."

"Since when is sleeping with a married man an issue with you?" Mary Beth snapped her verbal slap.

"Nate's not a man," Mandy scoffed. "He's not even a man-child."

"You've always hated him."

"At what point should I like him?" Mandy crossed her arms and glared. "After all he's done to you."

That was the one thing Mary Beth loved about her friends. It was why Case called them the Growing Strong Mafia. You hurt one, you hurt all. There were worse things in the world than to have one of your best friends as a sister.

Letting out a long breath Mary Beth steadied herself. "We need to talk."

"Since when?"

Mary Beth flopped on her couch and clutched a throw pillow to her chest.

"I assume Luke's asleep."

"I can care for small children, even when there isn't any Benadryl in the house. He loves his auntie." Mandy plopped in the overstuffed chair.

"About that." Mary Beth steeled herself. "I saw my dad today."

"So? Did he talk to you?"

"Um…eventually. He was with your mom."

"My mom? Why would my mom be with your dad? They haven't talked in years."

"Actually, they have." Mary Beth could hear her heart beat echoing through the room. "Did you know they were having an affair?"

"Bullshit. My mom's not sleeping with anyone. She still hasn't gotten over my father for some unknown reason."

"I know."

"Then you know she'd never sleep with anyone but him, wherever the hell he is."

"I know."

"Then how could—"

"Your mom's known my dad since before we were born," Mary Beth interjected to keep the focus on the whole story before reality crashed too hard against her skull and brought back the headache to end all headaches. "They lied when they said they met at our t-ball sign ups."

"Why would they do that?"

"Because he's your father."

"Fuck you. That's the meanest thing any of you bitches have ever said to me."

"That I'm your half-sister? Yeah, it's not the news I wanted today, but I think we both know my family is really good at disowning kids."

"I don't believe you."

"Right, because I make shit up all the time. Look at us. We're almost the same height, same build and the only difference in our eyes are the speckles."

Mandy looked at Mary Beth who could feel acid burning up her throat. Mandy wiped her eyes and crossed her arms.

"Is that why…why your mother has always scowled at me like I was gutter trash and refused to talk to my mom."

"I haven't talked to her, but I assume so."

"This is too much for me to process," Mandy said as she got up. Mary Beth caught her wrist.

"Tell me about it. Please don't run away. There's only one person in the entire world that can understand what I'm going through right now."

"So what," Mandy snapped. "I'm supposed to sit here and console you?"

"That's not what I meant." Mary Beth's stomach flipped and the sugar rush from the banana split was not helping her trembling hands. "I had a classic Mary Beth melt down at the restaurant." She sighed.

"What level," Mandy said through what had to be a closed off throat.

"I'd say it was a homer…oh crap, we never paid."

"They weren't going to rush after the crazy lady flailing her arms and biting the heads off chickens. Did you foam at the mouth again?"

"It wasn't a grand slam."

Mandy picked up the throw pillow and smacked Mary Beth across the face. They both fell to the couch, put their legs on the coffee table in unison, and burst into tear-filled laughter.

"I'm surprised your mom didn't pull you out of softball and toss you into dance or something."

"I guess when we all hit it off so well…it was the one thing that Dad wouldn't let her pull me out of. With Gabbie and Sarah around maybe she figured you'd be ostracized. She was a big enough bitch to your mom over the years."

"Sometimes my mom would cry after practices and games. I remember your mother getting other mothers to hate her too."

"I'm three months older than you. My father's a bastard."

"*Our* father's a bastard. Why the hell didn't he even acknowledge me? Did the asshole tell you that?"

"He wasn't really talking. I can only assume my mom's always had a strong hold on him. I guess your mom had worked in his office at the time. Something about getting scared after learning my mom was pregnant. *Your* mother was there to comfort him." As the words came out, Mary Beth could hear the condemnation in her tone.

"I'm sorry." With tears in her eyes she shook her head. "I wish I could get my mother's voice out of my head."

"There's one thing I think we both need."

"Eli already got me a banana split."

"No wonder you like him."

Mary Beth tossed the pillow at her.

"We need the girls."

That was something Mary Beth had to agree with. Even at twenty-four, sometimes you still need a sleepover to work on the big problems.

* * * *

Eli knocked on Mary Beth's door with two cups of coffee from Caribou, a bottle of ibuprofen, and a smile. Only Mary Beth didn't open the door. It was Maury's freight train of a daughter, Gabbie, if he remembered the name right. She was in pajama pants and an oversized T-shirt that read 'Fightin' Sioux Basketball'. Her black hair was pulled into a very disheveled ponytail flopped to the side of her head.

"Well, if it isn't the neighbor."

"The neighbor?" a high-pitched screech was followed by Mandy running into Gabbie's back and wrapping her arm around her waist. Both girls giggled and ogled him.

Mandy was in similar shape, except her T-shirt wasn't four sizes too big. It was skin-tight and her tits were bursting to escape the thin fabric. Now that he looked at her fully he could see the family resemblance. Sure Mandy's hair was dark brown and her skin tanned, but her facial structure and eyes had to be from her father.

"Move it, horn bags," a blonde said as she pushed the gigglers to the side. "Huh, that's what gets you heteros going? Thanks for the coffee." The blonde, who must be Sarah, said as she took his cup and walked back into the apartment.

"Is Mary Beth home?" Eli asked as he clutched the remaining cup to his chest.

"What are your intentions with my sister?" Mandy asked as she rested her head on Gabbie's shoulder.

"Intentions?"

"You want in…we want details. Do you have a 401-K? A degree? Long-term…you want kids?" Gabbie asked and right as Eli wondered what universe he'd landed in, Gabbie burst out laughing and she and Mandy fell back into the apartment.

"We couldn't help it," Mandy explained as she and Gabbie blocked his exit.

Dumb ass. He'd entered a vipers' nest. Right in the middle of making the sign of the cross, Eli saw his salvation. Luke. Thank God, he had an ally.

"Luke, save me."

"There's no escaping the mafia, my man," he said as if he'd be sorry to see him go in such a painful way. "Only one man has survived to live to tell the tale."

"What five-year-old talks like that?" Eli hitched his thumb to Luke and looked at the three women crashed on a couch with blankets and pillows strewn around the floor.

"You should hear my two-year-olds," Gabbie said. "There's something about being raised by the mafia that ages you...my man."

All the girls burst out in laughter again.

"What's so darn..." Mary Beth came out of the bathroom with just a towel wrapped around her chest.

Eli's jaw and her coffee dropped to the floor. She was rested, beautiful, and still had a few drops of water on her shoulders. Her normally pale skin was a light pink from the heat of the shower. The size of her pale yellow towel told him without a doubt her legs did go to Canada.

"I brought you some coffee." The words stumbled out of his dry mouth.

She looked down at the spilled drink and pulled in her lips.

"It smells wonderful. Too bad people are here or I'd drop this towel to mop up the mess."

"Oh no she didn't," Mandy scoffed. "Damn, you are my sister."

"Auntie, you said a swear," Luke chided.

"You are right, Luke. I think we need a jar so I stop my potty mouth."

Eli turned a full circle looking for the real Mary Beth. Who the hell was this woman?

"What did you do to Mary Beth?" he asked the gaggle sitting on the couch.

"Us?" Sarah said, holding her hand to her chest. "Um I'm pretty sure you brought the sextress out of her."

"Me?"

"Auntie Sarah, what's a set…sec…sectress?"

"It's a person who showers the second they get up." Sarah's quick response and authoritative tone almost had Eli believing the definition.

"Scared? There's the door," Mary Beth said as she stepped over the cup and got her paper towels. "I'm done putting up with people's BS."

"What's BS, Mama?"

"Baloney Scat. You gonna clean up your mess?" she asked, passing Eli the paper towels.

He took them, but grasped her wrist and pulled her to him. "I preferred your method."

The shock had finally worn off. Damn he was sprung on Mary Beth before. Now he'd never be able to get her out of his system.

She smiled up at him. "It was sweet of you to bring me coffee."

The timer buzzed on her stove.

"We made breakfast. Interested?"

"After I clean up."

Eli sat around with the girls eating an egg bake with Luke snuggled in next to his mother, who sadly got dressed in jeans and a sweatshirt. Even though Luke acted like a grown up there was a closeness between him and his mother that reminded Eli of his own mother. Luke knew something was wrong and not because his mother's friends had invaded their apartment. There was still the lost Mary Beth behind the public persona she was putting on for her girls. He'd be there for that Mary Beth, when the time came.

"To the championship." Gabbie raised a bite of egg bake in the air.

"The championship." The room joined in.

"Speaking of which, my uniform and children are at home."

"You left two-year-olds at home alone?"

"They're almost three and very smart," Gabbie said and grabbed a backpack. "And their father's at home."

As the girls all got up to leave Mary Beth gave a long hug to Mandy. They both appeared to be tearing up. Not that he blamed them.

"Eli, you're coming to the game right?" Sarah asked.

"Of course, Mary Beth asked me last night."

"Sextress strikes again. She just wants to show off her long legs…how far do they go? Roseville?"

"It's Canada bit…brat and you know it."

"Yeah, I always knew your cold butt had to be Canadian."

* * * *

At the game Eli was relegated to the Mafia bitches section, and bitches meant the men, one woman, and children of the girls. He met Case, Gabbie's husband, and their two-year-olds. Maury explained that Gabbie and Case adopted Case's younger siblings in May when they got married. Little Claire was a Mafioso in training yelling at the umps for her mommy and friends.

"Yeah, Momma…hit it…foul…foul…ump blind."

"Okay, little one," Maury said, as he happily flipped his granddaughter upside down.

"Now I see it, umps upside."

"She's two?" Eli asked.

"Almost three and I think you let her around her mother too much," Maury teased Case as he passed her back to Case's outstretched arms.

"I know. I wish I could tell Gabbie no once in a while, but she's got such a cute butt."

"That's my daughter," Maury warned.

"And a wonderful personality, too."

"Better."

Case was a taller guy with tight dreads pulled back by a binder. His mahogany eyes were a family trait both Claire and Charlie had. All three of the Thomas family were relegated to the bitch section had a deep chocolate brown complexion. Eli was told their romance could be turned into a blockbuster movie.

"Comedy spoof is more accurate," Case corrected his adoring father-in-law. "What's with you and the pitcher? Outside of Sarah's girl Lisa over there," Case pointed to a woman texting in the first row of the bleachers. "No one else has claimed any of the mafia."

"We're testing the waters."

"How they feeling?" Case asked.

"Warm, but choppy."

"Sounds right."

"You might want to tell your outfield to back up. You know you can't get a ball past me." One of the other team's players taunted Mary Beth as he stepped up to the plate. "Isn't that right, Mary—Hell?"

"Oh crapsticks," Maury said as he bounced Luke on his knee.

"You know him?"

"Yep. Hey, Luke, could you get old Maury a couple of hotdogs?"

"Yes." Luke seemed pleased to be thought of as big enough to complete the task.

"Awesome." With Luke tasked out to the concessions stand ten feet away, Maury grumbled, "That's one of Nate's friends. You know, Luke's dad. They're always tormenting Mary Beth and she falls for it every damn time."

"That is unless you've become a better pitcher than you are a mother," Nate's friend taunted.

Eli clenched his fist and stood up, but there was something on Mary Beth's face that looked like a match being lit. He'd seen it too much over the last few days.

With a loud thwack, followed by some expletives from Gabbie that had Case and Maury covering little ears, Mary Beth unleashed her fast-pitch. Gabbie stood up with the ball still in her glove as she hopped around. The ump stood dumbfounded and the whole stadium full of half-drunk softball players stared.

"You couldn't hit that in high school, Eric, and you still are a pussy when it comes to real softball. You want this to be a real championship? Or are you too scared?"

The batter stared her down while Gabbie pulled off her glove and Maury took off toward his truck.

"Here, hold Charlie and cover his ears...maybe for the rest of the game," Maury ordered and passed the little boy to Eli.

Eli instantly covered the boy's ears. At least he wasn't protesting like Claire was.

"Momma," Claire cried and Gabbie removed her facemask.

"I'm okay, Claire. Auntie Befs just surprised me. It's been a few years since I've had her throw that way to me."

"What's happening?" the ump asked. "Are we switching to fast-pitch or what?"

"It's up to the other team," Gabbie said as she took a three-inch thick sponge from her father. "I can handle the pitches now."

Gabbie held the sponge over her red and swelling palm as she pulled on her mitt.

"They're that hard?" the Ump mocked Gabbie.

"In high school she was clocked at a hundred and three miles per hour. So yeah, it smarts a little. Luckily the doctor said the pin he put in when she broke my hand the first time would keep it strong."

"The first time?"

"The doctor underestimated. So, Eric the Yellow Bellied Loud Mouth, we playing real ball or do we need to slow it down for you?" Gabbie taunted as she put her facemask on.

"Yeah, yellow," Claire yelled.

"Claire, what did Mommy say when she's playing ball?"

"Ta not listen talkin' smack."

"That's my girl."

"Fine," Eric the yellow snarled. "I can hit her wickedest pitch when I know it's coming."

"Really," Gabbie laughed. "Fine, I won't signal her. Send him the curve."

Gabbie got back into her stance and two more loud thwacks later Eric headed back to the dugout. Mary Beth looked like she had after her meltdown in her car.

Although the other team protested at first, Eric the stupid somehow convinced them to switch to fast-pitch. Big mistake. Eli couldn't believe how good the infield was on Mary Beth's team. Then again, with all but second base having played together since t-ball it shouldn't have been a shock. The few players that got a piece of Mary Beth's pitch learned quickly about the chemistry between them. Steals were quickly squelched. And the hits...damn. There was something sexy as hell to have a long legged woman knock the crap out of a ball.

Having won the league championship Eli waited at the edge of the backstop with the rest of the Mafia Bitches. It wasn't a bad place to stand, especially when Mary Beth sauntered over.

"Sorry it got a little heated." She shyly smiled at Eli. "Just seeking revenge on a few guys from high school."

"You were amazing." Eli reached for her hand.

Mary Beth took it without a thought and they went to Luke who'd been showing Charlie a trick he knew with his thumb.

"Ahhh...Mama," Charlie squealed as he ran to Gabbie. "Lukey's hurt. His tumb is gone."

"Is it really, because I found a thumb behind home-plate. You think it's his?"

Charlie was still unsure of what was going on while Gabbie "reattached" Luke's wandering thumb.

"Where'd he learn that?" Mary Beth asked.

"I got bored when you weren't the one hitting." Eli smiled.

Mary Beth turned into Eli's arms and wrapped his arm around her, never letting go of their interlaced fingers.

"Did you now?" She kissed him lightly and Eli knew he'd made headway with her.

"You want me to show you a few tricks tonight?"

"Maybe." She turned and called for Luke. "That game went a little late so Luke, we gotta get home to bed."

"She's right," Case added while holding the now passed out Claire. "She's gonna be so proud of you when she wakes up in the morning." Case beamed at Gabbie.

"For about two seconds, then she'll want pancakes."

"Probably. Good night all. Eli, it was nice to meet you. Hope to see you at the next MB gathering."

"Is there a support group?"

"Pretty much."

In the backseat Luke chattered away asking questions about the game and his mother's weird pitches. Mary Beth was attentive, but her hand did wander to Eli's and he couldn't have been happier.

When they arrived home, Luke rushed through the door to the apartment building first. Eli and Mary Beth walked a bit slower to enjoy the cool, late-September evening.

As Luke bound up the stairs, Eli turned and cupped Mary Beth's cheek. A strong kiss caught him by surprise as her soft lips embraced his and her arms wrapped around his neck.

"Daddy," Luke shrieked with joy when he hit the top step. Mary Beth froze.

Pulling back Eli could feel the instant disconnect as his body went from hot and wanton to cold and abandoned. Mary Beth walked up the stairs as if he were no longer with her.

"What are you doing here, Nate?" she asked.

Luke sat on Nate's hip. Eli took in his six-foot-three, large frame. He had Luke's blue eyes and blond hair—only Nate's was shorn down to less than an inch around his head. With broad shoulders and a muscular build Eli could understand how Mary Beth and Nate had been an attractive couple. If it wasn't for the tattoo sleeve on his right arm, Nate could have been the perfect example of the suburban white boy.

When Eli tried to place his hand on Mary Beth's back she stepped away. Eli attempted in vain to hold her hand. Instead of taking it she shook her head and gave a look that tore into his heart. She wanted him gone. No matter the reason Eli knew Nate had the upper hand when it came to Mary Beth.

Chapter Six

We must let go of the life we have planned,
so as to accept the one that is waiting for us.
                                                    —Joseph Campbell

"Who was that?" Nate asked as he stepped closer to Mary Beth.

"My neighbor," she replied, kicking herself for letting Eli go home.

"He seemed very...neighborly...is there something I should know?"

"No."

"Good."

Nate took another step closer and cupped Mary Beth's cheek. All she could think of was Eli and how good he'd smelled after the game. Nate stroked her cheekbone and leaned in for a kiss. She turned her head and pulled back.

"It confuses Luke," she explained.

"What?" Nate asked as his warm breath tickled her ear. "To see his mom and dad kissing? That's what kids want to see, isn't it?" He licked along her neck and she squirmed from his hold.

"Why are you here?"

"Eric said he lost his game to you today. I thought I'd come congratulate you." Nate spun Luke around and he giggled in glee, then Nate placed him back on the floor. "Did Mommy win her game today, Lukey?"

"What, are you on every jerk from high school's speed dial?"

"I miss watching you really play." Nate pressed her against the door. His hand landed on her breast and then slid down the side of her body until he landed at her hip. "You gonna let me in?"

"Not tonight. It's late and Luke has school in the morning."

"I know it's Luke's bedtime," Nate growled against her cheek as his hand went to cup her ass.

"Nate, not tonight."

"You know no one will ever love you like I do."

"I know." She broke from his clutches and turned the key in the lock. "I've got to get Luke to bed."

"I'll help." Nate pressed his body against Mary Beth's back and whispered, "You wouldn't deny a father the right to put his son to bed would you?"

Anger tore through her body hitting every muscle and making them tense in revulsion. Nate wasn't a father. He used this excuse anytime Mary Beth wanted space.

"He's not going to marry you?" her mother had squealed. *"Not surprising. You gave him what he wanted without making him take responsibility. I'm amazed he hasn't asked you to abort it."* He had, that's what made her mother's condemnation worse. *"You better hope he'll step up and be a father, because you can't raise a child without one."*

"No." Mary Beth's voice trembled as a headache emerged behind her right eye, but she couldn't let go. Nate hated emotional outbursts. He found them juvenile and repulsive.

"You got him in and out of the bath that quick?" she asked as she finished loading the last of the breakfast dishes in the dishwasher.

"He doesn't need a bath," Nate said as he saddled up behind her and pressed his already erect penis against her backside. "I on the other hand could use a long shower with the sexiest pitcher this side of the Mississippi. What do you say? You think you could wash some *hard* to reach parts for me?"

"Where's Carrie?"

"I don't care." Nate nibbled on Mary Beth's collarbone as his voice vibrated down her spine. "You're who I care about."

"Then why'dja marry her?"

Nate stilled behind Mary Beth for a moment.

"Don't do this shit. You think I like cheating on my wife with you? I wish she did to me what you do, but she doesn't. You're who I want, I just can't be married to you. You know that, right? We're great in bed and good with Lukey, but otherwise we suck."

Mary Beth turned in his arms and scowled at him.

"So I'm the one you want to go down on you, and she's the one you want to…what do you do together? Neither of you seem the conversational type."

"Don't start with me, Mary Beth. If I wanted to fight about nothing, I'd go home to Carrie."

"Why don't you? A hole's a hole or is that what you just say to those geniuses you have on speed dial that still worship the guy who played three whole games in the minors before getting cut."

"Don't bring that up. You don't know what it's like to…"

"Have responsibilities? To have to perform every day even when you're exhausted? To chase a dream even though no one is looking?"

"I hurt my knee."

"It works pretty damn well when you're on it begging me for a piece."

"I never need to beg with you."

Mary Beth slapped him so fast and hard her hand stung before she'd registered the sound of the hit.

"I'm so sorry." She brought her hands to her face and felt her world fading around her. "Please, Nate, please forgive me. I didn't mean…"

His eyes darkened as his head moved back slowly to look at her. There was a red mark, but he didn't even touch it. Instead, his top lip curled.

"You know what I want. There's only one way to get it. Let's see how your knees held up after your game."

"Nate, I don't want to."

"Oh, you don't want my forgiveness?" Nate claimed her lips in a hard forceful kiss that Mary Beth, for once, noticed there was only his desire behind—not love—like she'd been deluding herself.

Mary Beth fought the tears pricking the edge of her eyes.

"No. No she doesn't." Eli stood holding Luke's hand by the island. "And she sure as heck doesn't need it."

"Daddy?" Luke called, and Nate's face twitched.

70

"This is a family matter." Nate kept his eyes trained on Mary Beth. "Get out. And take Luke with you. His mommy and daddy have some things they need to straighten out."

Nate's eyes still trapped Mary Beth. She wanted to pull away. She wanted to break the spell he always had on her, but couldn't. His forgiveness. His approval. His love was… Who was she kidding? She mused. He didn't love her.

"Eli, how did you get Luke?" Mary Beth asked, breaking away from Nate for the first time—ever.

Once in the gaze of Eli's obsidian eyes she felt safe to rage, safe to protect her body, and most importantly safe to break free to love someone else. Sadly, she also saw disappointment and hurt looking back at her.

"He came to my apartment wanting me to read him a story since he didn't get one."

"You don't need a story," Nate said with his condescending tone. "I told you to go to sleep."

"You always say to sleep. I'm not," Luke yawned, "Sleepy."

"Looks like you are to me little man." Nate tussled Luke's hair. "Now head on back to bed."

"No. I want a story. Mommy always reads me a story so I don't have nigh'mares."

"How 'bout Daddy goes in your room and kills the monster in your closet so you won't have nightmares?"

"Mama!" Luke screeched and clung to Eli's leg.

"Jesus, Mary, and Joseph, Nathan! Are you trying to scare the crap out of him?" Mary Beth scooped Luke up in her arms and carried him to his bedroom. "Your dad's an idiot. He wouldn't know a monster from a hole in his butt. I got a monster free apartment, Lukey."

* * * *

Eli glared at Nate. He wasn't sure which situation pissed him off more. Right now the only person in this apartment he could stand was Luke. What the hell did Nate offer Mary Beth? Was she a sicko that wanted a man to lord over her? Make her beg for forgiveness for doing nothing more than stopping a man from forcing her into sex? Forget this shit. There was a lot he could handle, but this…he couldn't. No, this he would not.

"You need to leave," Nate ordered.

Eli crossed his arms and rested against the wall.

"Really?" Nate scoffed. "You think you could take me?"

Eli learned a long time ago, against bullies, silence speaks volumes.

"What? You no *habla ingels*?"

Eli shifted his weight and sighed.

"What's your problem, man?" Nate growled as his nostrils flared.

"I'm just making sure your son, who clung to me when he was scared, gets to sleep. After that, whatever sick twisted shit you and Mary Beth have going can continue."

"You're not fucking her are you?"

"I'm here for my little friend. Mary Beth's a big girl, she can protect herself."

Nate rushed Eli and pinned him by his neck to the wall with his forearm.

"What are you? A pedophile? Going after a single mother and her son. I swear to God you lay one finger on my son—"

Eli swept Nate's legs and let his big ass drop to the floor before Eli used his knee to pin Nate down.

"At least you care about one of them."

"She's mine. Always has been, always will be. I don't need Luke. Even without him she'd still be with me. I own her. Heart and soul."

There it was laid out for him.

Mary Beth came out and stared at the two of them. Eli couldn't read her well enough to know if it was anger, fear, or gratitude on her face. Maybe it was just plain old shock.

"Forget it." Eli pressed his knee hard as he got up. "Luke asleep?"

"He was, I'm not sure if he still is after the earthquake, but he should be fine."

"Good." Eli headed to his apartment.

"Wait…" Mary Beth called just as he was at his door.

"I don't have time for this, Mary Beth."

Eli closed his door and wished he hadn't seen the hurt in Mary Beth's hazel eyes. That he could read. Too damn well. Maybe because it was her normal look and sadly the only time he'd seen it gone was when she was in his arms. That was the only difference between her and Isabella. He just wished it was enough.

The next day Elias pulled up to the one and a half story house on the East Side of St Paul, his mother was outside washing the front bay window. Her short bob of black hair was pulled back on the right side with a bobby pin or two just like when he was five. She never changed. She was his constant. No, she was his father's constant. Had been for almost forty years now. No wonder he was a damn romantic sappy *oso chiquito*. His brothers were right—he was a damn tenderhearted teddy bear. Frickin' Care Bears.

When his mother saw him coming up their walkway she wiped her hands on the dishtowel of death and smiled at him. Even greeted him at the door with a hug and kiss on his cheek.

"This is a nice surprise," she said as they walked into the kitchen. Today she'd been cooking. He could tell by the mess on the counter and the delicious smell of tamales wafting from the oven. "I wish you would have told me you were coming, I used the last of my *Masa*."

"Did you have enough to make a full batch?"

"I made two actually."

"Two?" Eli lit up at the idea he'd be able to have leftovers.

"Yes, to freeze a batch for your sister," she replied with a raised eyebrow. "Don't worry, you know my batches are based on a full house not a half full one."

Thankfully, his mother hadn't learned how to cut her cooking. After years of cooking for a family of seven he'd lucked out, but that could also explain his little paunch. His hand circled his belly and remembered how lean Nate was.

"Where's Jesus?"

"He's running."

"Running?"

"The distance sport, he's at practice."

"Cross-country? Jesus is running cross-country?"

"Yes, didn't he tell you?"

"No, because I would have asked what her name was."

73

"I believe it's Ebony," his mother's knowing smile told Eli she knew everything. "I was surprised. He must really like her to pass up soccer this year. Then again, he wasn't as good as you were."

"That's true, which means as a junior being stuck bench warming on JV would be embarrassing."

"You boys, at least you tried." She giggled and pulled the warm tamales out of the pot.

Serving three to Eli and two for herself, she sat down at the kitchen table and held his hand as they both bowed their heads and prayed over the food. A necessary concession he thought as the warm steam curled up off the plate and assaulted his olfactory senses like a stripper on a pole. His mouth watered as he tried to focus on the task at hand, which was...oh yeah, thanking God for his mother's ability to cook and for always being here for him.

That thought alone made him take an extra minute before he said amen. Mary Beth couldn't go home and have her mother cook her favorite childhood meal. Hell, she wouldn't even cook her least favorite that would still be comforting because it came from her mother. She wouldn't hold Mary Beth's hand and bless her food for her. She wouldn't give her a hug and tell her she loved her. How would that feel? Eli looked at his mother who knew there was something more than his stomach aching.

Her head tilted to the side as if that made it easier for her to hear his problems. His mother always met her kids exactly where they needed to be met. With his sister he'd always feared she was being run over, but she wasn't. With him she'd squeeze his hand to say it was okay to unload. She'd wait patiently, not saying a thing, just looking at him. If he talked she'd listen, if he stayed silent she would too, knowing full well he'd break eventually.

He got up from his chair and wrapped his arms around her and she took him into her caring embrace. He was Tender Heart Bear. Here he'd been worried coming in second in Mary Beth's heart—he never thought about the fact she'd never been first in anyone's. Ever. How could she return a love she'd never known? Even her father who she thought put her first abandoned her.

Sitting back down, Eli tried to pull on his man pants and quit being such a pussy.

"I thought you said you weren't seeing anyone, Elias."

"The situation changed, Mama. There was a miscommunication. The girl wasn't married."

"Ah, then why are you hugging me like Isabella has just been beaten to death again?"

"I'm not crying," he mumbled as he sat back down and finally took a bite of his tamale that melted in his mouth. Just the right amount of cumin and a dozen other spices his mother would never divulge for fear he and his siblings would stop showing up…or at least that's the excuse she used.

"No, but something is wrong."

"Her name is Mary Beth and we did go out a few times."

"Did she say she didn't want to see you anymore?"

"No. But she has a son from a previous relationship."

His mother inhaled sharply, and then settled herself down again.

"He's five, well, almost six."

"Six? How old is this woman?"

"She's my age. She got pregnant in high school." Eli looked up from his plate of comfort food and felt the need to explain more. "Mama, she owns her own business and is in school. She's a wonderful mother, although she can't see it, but—"

"You don't have to explain your choices to me. Although if you get involved with her you're getting involved with him. Are you ready to be a father overnight?"

"He's great, actually." He smiled broadly as if he had some claim on Luke's accomplishments. "Smart as heck too."

"Explain the problem."

"His father."

His mama gave a knowing mmm. "It is hard. It's not like a past boyfriend you run into at the movies. He'll always be around."

"I think she still loves him."

"Then she can't love you. Not really. And my *oso chiquito* deserves someone who loves him."

The backdoor opened and his dad came through. His mother instantly got up and prepared a plate for him. With a smile she set it down at his seat as he washed the day's dirt off his hands. Worn out from a day working on his uncle's construction crew Eli watched the silent conversation between his mother and father. His dad acknowledged his presence with a smile of peace and began eating. His dark skin was wrinkled around his tired eyes and his hair was finally showing his age as salt now peppered his dark hair.

"Good evening, Elias."

"Good evening, Papa."

For a moment he thought his father would say more, but he didn't need to. Everyone in their family knew his good evening was the same as saying I love you and I'm so happy to see you. That was his father. Quiet, reserved, and just as tender hearted as Eli. Eli just had his mother's mouth so everyone made fun of him for it.

"What are you going to do? Is she one you fight for?"

"When we're together…"

"*Oso chiquito's* in love again?" his father's soft, but commanding voice resonated in the room even though he hadn't raised his head from the plate.

It made both Elias and his mother turn. Even with Isabella his dad had kept silent. He was always silent.

"If you love her, make your demands known early."

"My demands? Who makes demands in a relationship?"

His dad slowly raised his head and stared across the table at him. The obsidian eyes he'd inherited were stern.

"Men who go after and keep their women."

His father then returned to his plate of food and didn't speak again.

Chapter Seven

I believe that every single event in life happens in an opportunity to choose love over fear.
—Oprah Winfrey

Mary Beth stared at her computer for over an hour. Her finger rolled the mouse up and down the page just enough so it didn't time out. There was information she needed from the AMI, Association Montessori Internationale, on accreditation. The other page she clicked on was about the State of Minnesota's licensing for schools. It didn't matter what they said—Mary Beth's eyes couldn't process a thing.

A knock on her door woke her up.

"Isn't it time to get Luke?"

"Huh?" Mary Beth woke as she turned to Sarah.

"Friday? Awesome mom time."

Mary Beth looked in the corner of her computer to see it was almost two-thirty.

"I have a few minutes."

"Hey, what's going on? You've been grumpy all week. We assumed it was getting used to Mandy as your sister, but you two haven't even really talked since Sunday."

"No, we haven't. Mandy and I weren't the closest to begin with, thanks to my mom. But she's not what's distracting me."

"Then what?"

"Nate said no man will love me like he does."

"Gabbie said you didn't want our opinion of him. And why are you thinking about him. Don't you have neighbor boy?"

"I haven't seen Eli all week...not since..."

Michel Prince

Mary Beth closed out the windows on her computer and powered it down for the weekend. Pushing back, she looked up at Sarah whose hair showed signs of heavy-duty time on the playground. She had at least three leaves stuck in her ponytail.

"Let me clean you up," Mary Beth teased and pulled the dried leaves out.

"Since when, Mary Beth?" Sarah held her hands.

"Since Sunday night."

"He didn't?" Sarah sighed. "Damn, I thought Eli was a good guy."

"He is. What do you think he did?"

"Sleep with you, then never call."

"He didn't sleep with me. Nate was at my door when I got home."

Sarah's face dropped and she ran her hand over her eyes and down her face. "What did you do?" she accused.

"I didn't do anything."

"Really. You turned down Nate."

"Yes, I even kicked him out of my house...eventually." Adding the last part a bit under her breath.

"Did you invite Eli in?"

"Not in time." Mary Beth let out a sigh and tossed her hands up. "Luke ran to his apartment and brought him back. He caught Nate and I."

"Doing what?"

"I'm not sure."

"How do you not know what you did?"

"I don't know when he walked in. I think he missed the slap."

"Nate hit you." Sarah slammed her fist down on Mary Beth's desk. "I'll castrate him."

"I hit Nate," Mary Beth admitted sheepishly.

"You? You don't hit anything."

"I've been doing a lot of things I don't usually do."

"Like what?"

"Like making out in a parking lot with my loan guy and telling Nate no."

"Both sound positive to me."

"I really like him."

"Eli, right?"

"Yeah." Mary Beth nervously fiddled with her pen.

"Then how about I come over after work and deal with the spawn."

"That helps me how?"

"You sit outside Eli's apartment until he lets you in."

"Because stalker is the new black?"

"Works in all the movies."

"Oh well in that case it's foolproof." Mary Beth got up and grabbed her bag. "It was just easier in high school. I knew the rules and who the players were."

"Yet you still let Nate impregnate you."

"You saying I've been this dumb since high school?"

"And the little lady wins a prize."

"Brat."

"You want me to stop by tonight?"

"Yes, but bring some hard lemonade just in case he refuses to open his door to me."

"Deal."

After picking up Luke from school, Mary Beth hit a Super Target in hopes of finding a grown up outfit to accent any part of her. Finding an emerald green wrap dress on clearance from summer, she prayed she remembered her shoe collection correctly. This would be perfect to accent her hair and eyes, and it fit in a way she'd never known a dress could.

"You look pretty, Mama," Luke said after he turned around in the dressing room. "You going somewhere 'pecial?"

"I…well…" Mary Beth had never really thought about dating other people with a child.

Surely it couldn't be good for kids to have multiple men coming in and out of their lives. Then again Nate didn't think that while dating for the few years before marrying Carrie.

"I wanted to thank Eli for bringing you back to be tucked in right. We never really talked about that. Why did you go to Eli's apartment?"

"I don't know."

"Luke, there had to be a reason you just didn't ask me."

"Daddy said not to interrupt kissing grown ups."

"But Daddy and I weren't kissing."

"You were going to."

"How do you know?"

"'Cuz Daddy always kisses you." Luke's eyes looked up with pure innocence.

"Do you see us kiss?"

"Sometimes. I don't take naps. I'm almost six."

"Yeah, you are a big guy. What would you think if Mommy kissed Eli?"

"You kiss all my aunties."

"On their cheeks. Not what I was asking."

"Well, Daddy kisses Carrie."

"Yes he does."

"What's the difference?"

And there it was, directly from the mouth of her baby.

* * * *

"So, you like her, just not enough to fight for her," Eddie grumbled at Eli on the phone. His father finds out and suddenly everyone knows.

"Why should I have to fight for her?"

"Because you want her and for the first time ever you're telling me about things that don't include positions you could bend her into."

"What's that supposed to mean?" Eli growled.

"It means, most times when you describe a woman to me you talk about her ass, hips, or tits. You then gloat about how fast you got her naked or how many times you came. So far you've talked about Mary Beth's business, crazy family, and the fact you didn't mind being known as *her* bitch at a softball game. Which means either you didn't even kiss her, or you actually respect the woman."

Damn, Eli hated when Eddie was right. Eli didn't gloat to anyone but Eddie and vice versa. Before Eddie met Sophia, they'd kept a running list of conquests. Now if it wasn't for the fact she was currently four months pregnant, Eli would have never known Eddie ever got laid.

"I shouldn't have to chase her."

"Because she's just supposed to show up at your door and—"

A knock made Eli drop the phone. Scrambling he picked it up off the floor and headed to the door.

"Someone's at my door."

"Who?" Eddie teased.

All Eli saw through the peephole was a flash of red.

"Man, it's her…what the hell do I do?" Eli asked as panic racked his whole body.

Maybe it wasn't her. Maybe it was a pizza delivery guy at the wrong address. Eli peered through again and saw a form fitting green dress. The distortion of the peephole made Mary Beth's breasts scream his name. Oh, man what he wanted to do to those. No. She chose her ex over him. He wasn't going to fight…one more little peek. Damn that woman. Her finger glided just under the emerald green fabric above her left breast as if she were trying to smooth something out. He'd love to smooth something…and he was hard as a fucking brick…great, now he couldn't answer the door.

She knocked again and when he looked for the third time she was biting her bottom lip. Disappointment and worry crossed her face and he couldn't fight the urge to use her lip for a much more delicious reason.

"You answering that, or do you want to keep crying on the phone to me?"

"I'm getting it, I'm getting it…I just…you should see the dress she has on. No, on second thought, you shouldn't."

"I knew you liked her. Bye-bye, *oso chiquito*."

"I hate you," Eli said into the phone, but also as he opened the door.

Mary Beth looked as if she'd been slapped as she turned away.

"Wait. What did you want?"

"Nothing. It was a mistake."

"Mary Beth, stop." She turned around to look at him.

"I understand why you hate me. I was wrong the other day. I wanted to see if there was a way I could say I was sorry."

"I don't force women to seek my forgiveness." Eli crossed his arms and leaned against the doorjamb. "It's not my style."

"Do you forgive?" She asked as she pressed her toe into the carpet.

"Why aren't you wearing any shoes?"

"I didn't have any to match and I was just going a few doors down...I guess I thought the dress was more important than my shoes."

Eli arched an eyebrow at her. She thought right. The sheer material of her green dress clung to her body, wrapping around her with a nice V cut between her breasts. The skirt hugged her tight little butt, then fanned out until it reached her knees. In her hands was a reusable grocery bag that didn't quite go with the outfit, but, as she'd said, it was all about the dress.

"What's in the bag?"

"I made supper, got a sitter, and hoped you wouldn't mind sharing a meal without a show ten minutes in."

"Dinner without a show..." Eli acted as if he was pondering the idea, but really he was scanning her curves and trying to squelch these stupid feelings of letting her into his life.

"I left my phone at home. There is only one person over the age of eighteen who'll know where to reach me in case of an emergency. She even said she'd spend the night if I..."

Spend the night... Awe, man...

"Well, if you're not interested."

"Tell me one thing."

"Anything," Mary Beth promised.

"What were you trying to be forgiven for?"

"I may have slapped Nate and told him I didn't want to sleep with him."

"What, has the guy never heard the word no from you?"

"Not really. Once," she began, then silenced herself. "Otherwise...he's always had a power over me. Even after he got married."

"He's married?"

Mary Beth pulled into herself as she took a few steps back.

"Yeah, I'm not proud of that."

"You said had. What changed?"

Mary Beth rocked on her feet as her lips knitted to hide a smile.

"I learned how it's supposed to feel when you're kissed."

"Did you now?"

"And I didn't think I should have to settle. I didn't want to settle. I wanted someone who kissed me as if they cared about me. I want someone who doesn't get upset when I go a little crazy."

"A man like that exists in the world?" Eli mocked.

"It surprised me too."

"So, who do you know that kisses like that?"

Mary Beth slowly sauntered over to Eli. She pointed her toes to make her long legs even longer. The only appetite he had at the moment was for the soft flesh of this woman.

"Well, you see…" She smiled. "I have this chatty neighbor…"

"Do you now? Chatty, you say?"

Her hand curled around the top of his shirt as she pulled herself to him.

"Very, at least around me. Maybe he just wanted to show off how talented his tongue is."

"Could be." Eli's lips tingled as the subtle scent of woman rose from Mary Beth's neck.

"He's got the most amazing tongue and lips."

"A twofer."

"Mmm…" she growled as she pressed her hip against him and felt his hardness. "This thing always seems to be around."

"Would you prefer if it never surfaced?"

"I don't know…" Mary Beth pulled back and he could see the mask she wore when her friends were there eating breakfast.

"What don't you know, Mary Beth?" Eli asked as he leaned in close and pressed her body against the doorjamb.

"My head is all muddled right now."

"With what?"

"I really want to…well…you know, but…"

"Is this that Catholic guilt thing again?"

"A little bit."

"The sextress, is that the impulsive you that you try to hide?"

Mary Beth looked him in the eye and he could see her trying to calculate something in her head.

"Stop," he ordered, and she steeled herself. "I'm not here to judge you."

Eli brought his finger to the top of her forehead and traced along her hairline until he found a few strands long enough to tuck behind her ear. Mary Beth trembled against his touch and Eli moved closer to whisper.

"Saint or sinner I want you in my life. You're all I can think about. The way you knit your forehead when you're about to explode and the way your eyes get brighter when Luke's around. Get out of your head and we can see how this night goes. If you want to be the sextress, I'm not going to judge you. You want to be a nun until marriage I'd still love to eat…" Eli smiled and bit his bottom lip, "what you brought me, but don't bottle up your feelings or put on some damn fake persona you think I want. Mary Beth, the only thing I want from you, is you."

Fire began to burn in Mary Beth's eyes as she sprung for Eli's lips. The heat of her kiss sent them tumbling into his apartment as they locked in the embrace. The bag of food slipped off her arm and crashed to the floor, but neither acknowledged the possible disaster as they somehow managed to find a hard surface to land on. Sure, it was the table, but at least now Mary Beth was sprawled on top of a surface and Eli could engulf her body with his.

Caressing her lips gently to tease until he could once again claim them fully, she rubbed herself against his hardened shaft. How he wanted to travel down her body and taste every inch of her, but the want and need of both of them turned into a passion that would have destroyed dishware if they'd set the table first.

In a fury, Mary Beth's hands went to his belt as he traveled to her neck with wet kisses. A quick yank brought the strap of her dress down her arm and exposed her perfect, alabaster breast and its soft, pink nipple and erect peak. His mouth surrounded the hardened flesh right as she released him from the confines of his pants.

Mary Beth moaned as her head fell back and Eli braced her back with his hand. With lips fused on her nipple he sucked the swollen flesh as she began to stroke his engorged shaft with her long fingers.

"Eli please," she cried. "Take me."

He wasn't going to just take her. He was going to devour her heart and soul. With his free hand he found his way under her skirt, brushed aside the lacey thong, and found her delicate folds. Wet and wanton, he had to release her breast from his lips to stem the tide of his release.

"Let go of me, Mary Beth," he panted. "I don't want to come yet and your soft fingers are..." she stroked to the top of his cock and her fingers tickled the tip then moved to hold onto his shoulders. "Woman," he growled.

Sliding two fingers inside Mary Beth, he placed his thumb on her clit to create a counter rotation. A little trick he'd learned years ago. His fingers rotated right as his thumb went to the left. It kept him focused on the task at hand and allowed him to stop from coming all over the table.

Mary Beth looked up at him with sweat already beading her forehead. Her lips were swollen as she panted through an orgasm that caused ripples against his fingers.

"That's my girl. I want to see that pretty white cream come out of you."

"What?" she moaned.

"You're coming aren't you?"

"Yes." Mary Beth's head bucked back as her hips thrust hard against his hand. "Oh God yes."

"That's it. Come for your man."

Eli felt the ripples in her core begin to slow down.

"You want more, Mary Beth? You want me inside you?"

"Yes," she moaned. "Please Elias."

Oh the way her mouth formed his name made his dick twitch and his heart quicken.

"Will you wait for me here?"

"Don't leave me," she begged and opened her eyes. The green was sparkling even through sated eyes. "Please don't leave me."

"Do you want a little Latino baby in the next nine months?"

"Oh, I'm...thank you."

"I just have to go to my room. You want to come with me?"

"I would if my legs still worked."

Eli smiled and kissed her lips tenderly.

"You really haven't been touched right by a man."

Mary Beth scooted back on the table and smoothed her skirt down her legs.

"I'm going to need to go back to carrying protection," Eli growled.

"Did you have it when we went car shopping?"

"No. I wanted to be with you, but carrying seemed premature."

"You don't think I'm easy do you?" Mary Beth slid off his table on her wobbly legs. "I'm not you know."

Eli wrapped his arms around her and cradled her head so they were touching nose to nose.

"I don't. I just think you and I have a combustible draw to each other."

"Do we?"

"Let me tell you, I didn't see the same look when you were in the hallway with Nate as you had waiting at my door."

"You bring out something in me, Elias Marquez. I've been doing all sorts of new things. It must be your eyes."

"These little things?" Eli said as he licked his lips and kept his eyes locked on hers.

For a moment Mary Beth came out of her sextress ways. Her hands cradled his head and Eli could see tears pooling.

"No one has ever accepted me. I'm always playing the role of good mother, big sister or loyal girlfriend. I've never been allowed to scream and not be chastised for it. Be sexy and not get laughed at for my attempt. By playing along and acting—"

"I'm not acting."

"Even better, you accept me and I've never known that before from anyone. The worst part is I have three great friends who strangely accept that I'm always in the pleasing mode, but would love if I had more than just a few wild outbursts."

"You wouldn't have outbursts if you'd just be yourself."

"But what if no one wanted me anymore."

"Only the ones who didn't want you in the first place would turn their backs to you. In my family, we never cared what the Jones' had or if they thought we were something bad or good. When I look at you," Eli's hand slid down Mary Beth's leg and wrapped it around his waist. Pulling her hips to him she smiled. "I see an amazingly sexy woman. I have since the first day. A caring, yet overwhelmed mother. An amazing friend. And most importantly, a pretty strong person."

"I'm not—"

Eli wasn't going to let her self-doubt squeak back in, especially when she was in a very hot dress, and he'd already had her panting. With viper like swiftness he reclaimed the lips he'd been missing since she walked away from him a week ago and decided he'd never let those lips leave him again.

* * * *

"Maybe we should have dinner first," Eli suggested when he released her from the most amazing kiss Mary Beth had ever known.

"Dinner?" Mary Beth whimpered. "You want dinner?"

"I'd rather gut out the pain in my groin as I keep you on edge for a little while longer." Eli tucked himself back in behind his zipper. Damn it, he was just what she needed. Not that Mary Beth needed sex in the grand scheme of things, but he had every nerve in her body tweaked.

"That's just mean."

"You've already come once, who's really at a disadvantage here?"

Mary Beth's heart beat like a rock drummer and every nerve in her body ached. Sure, she'd come, from fingers…not the same thing. She wanted a hard shaft inside her thrusting over and over until she couldn't see straight. A sore want built and with every shift in weight her panties rubbed against the engorged flesh, sending it to another level of torture.

"What if I lose the mood?"

Eli's dark eyes sparkled as he leaned in close, bringing his damn accent when he did.

"Tell the truth. How often when it's just you and me are you out of the mood?"

Mary Beth held her breath as she licked her lips.

"That's what I thought." He rubbed his nose against hers and she had to catch herself from falling to the ground. "What did you make me, *mi reina*?"

"Me what?"

"*Mi reina*. It just means you're mine." Eli let his finger glide down her arm, barely caressing her flesh. "Do you want to be mine?"

The drummer inside Mary Beth's heart decided it was time for a solo. The loud pounding of her heart echoed throughout her whole body and she swore the world had stopped.

87

Be his? It seemed so much more than just boyfriend-girlfriend conversation. Could she give up Nate forever? Or for as long as she and Elias were together? Sure she'd said no to Nate once for Eli...but it wasn't for Eli—it was for herself.

Eli's finger had reached her wrist and was softly returning up her arm.

"So," he whispered. "Will you be *mi reina*?"

Mary Beth's lips were filled with tingling sensations as she wrapped her arms around his neck and found the combustible heat that always happened with him. Their tongues met in a battle for control and Eli fell back as his arms wrapped around her waist. Falling down into the living room, they both turned toward his bedroom and Mary Beth was thankful the layout for his apartment was the same as hers.

The threat of teasing her during dinner seemed to have evaporated as Eli pulled the string on her dress and completely exposed her body to him. Her straps fell down her arms as she abandoned her dress to the floor. Falling back on the bed Eli scanned her body, only covered by a small, nude colored thong. When her hands attempted to cover her breasts Eli snatched her by the wrist and brought her body on top of his.

"Woman, even if I didn't already speak Spanish you'd have me talking in tongues tonight."

Again Mary Beth unleashed his manhood as his pants joined her dress on the floor. Popping the buttons on his shirt, she found his strong upper body and his little paunch of a belly. Mary Beth licked at his belly button as she slid her tongue up to his nipple and nipped it with her teeth.

"*Wo ist das kondom?*"

"I think I heard condom?"

"*Ich spreche Deutsch.*"

"You speak German." Eli laughed.

"What can I say, you already have me speaking in tongues."

"I haven't even begun." Eli flipped Mary Beth over in his bed and then reached for his nightstand drawer.

Placing the condom on the pillow next to her head Eli nuzzled against her neck and worked his way down the center of her chest. His strong hands held her breasts as they kneaded the now sore flesh and tweaked her erect nipples. Still his mouth traveled until he reached her belly and he looked up with a devilish grin. His hands released her breasts and his fingers locked on either side of her thong to remove it.

When he kissed right above her hairline gooseflesh erupted up her body and she feared she might have bit off more than she could chew. Then again, considering when she held him in the kitchen, she had a handful in general.

"You still haven't answered me," Eli said as he blew on Mary Beth's engorged clit.

"Answered you?" she asked as she squirmed from the sensation. "Was there a question?"

"I asked if you'd be *mi reina*? Will you be mine alone?"

His accent was back and she didn't want to be ruled by her hormones.

"Can you ask me again when I'm not on the verge of explosion?"

"When you have a level head you mean?"

"Yes."

"Because in this moment the answer is yes?"

"Without a doubt."

"How many states away do I have to be to not have you turned on?"

That was a good question. Mary Beth had been finding herself thinking about Eli like it was an Olympic sport.

"I'm about to say something really nasty and out of character."

Eli smirked and arched his right eyebrow.

"Quit being a girl and fuck me like a man."

* * * *

God damn, he loved Mary Beth's fire.

Taking her command as if he had no other option, he brought his mouth to her sex and found the sweetest flavor still covering her from her last orgasm. With the swollen bud inside his lips, his tongue reached and flicked it.

"Jesus, Eli!" Mary Beth bucked her hips and he took her fully into his mouth.

With deep explorations of his tongue he did what he was told to. He fucked his *reina* with his tongue until she tugged his hair and demanded he stop torturing her.

"I've seen what you're packing, Eli," Mary Beth growled as she looked down between her thighs. "Please…"

He could feel her orgasm shuddering against his tongue with each stroke. His balls tightened at the thought of ripples gripping him and he knew as much as she needed him, he needed her more. Reaching for the condom, he sheathed himself and climbed up her body.

Locking her right leg over his arm, he spread her legs further and rammed his shaft inside, riding the last of her orgasm until he reached the hilt. Pulling her body tightly to his, she clung to his shoulders and he thrust inside her.

"Who's your man, Mary Beth?" he whispered against her neck as her legs locked on to his hips. "That's it, baby. Hold on."

Eli rotated his hips and when he felt her tightening around him once more he pulled back just enough to pound inside in quick short bursts.

"Who, Mary Beth?" he groaned as he braced himself against the headboard.

"You are. Oh, Elias," she cried. The ripples surrounded his shaft and Eli couldn't hold back any longer.

The way she moaned 'Elias' as if he were the answer to her prayers caused his mind to spin as his balls tightened and ass clenched. He poured all he had inside him into Mary Beth. With a fevered kiss, he tried to hold back the love and devotion, but he sputtered until nothing was held back. The emotional attachment he'd feared and longed for changed the sex into something more. Something very much more than he'd ever experienced. And as they both fell to the bed in utter exhaustion, Eli knew his heart was no longer his own.

Her firm thighs had yet to release his hips and her arms clung to him. A light misting of sweat covered the two of them. When he looked down at her still lying beneath him, their eyes locked and he could see his future playing out like a movie.

Three little kids bounded between the green speckles in her eyes and Luke chased them around the backyard at Eli's mother's house. Eli scooped up the smallest one who called him Papa and demanded he be allowed to keep playing with his big brother Lukey. Maybe they weren't all his, but then again the thought of children with Mary Beth had him sighing.

He could see Mary Beth walking out with a serving dish as she chatted away with his mother and sister. His whole family accepted her and when he leaned against the small deck in the backyard his dad put his arm around Eli's shoulders and told him he had a good looking family.

It could all be so simple if she'd just…Eli didn't want to fall down the rabbit hole again. He wasn't going to let himself dream of what could be until he knew she would be his.

Steadying himself he stroked Mary Beth's flushed cheek and planted a light kiss on her nose.

"So, what's for dinner?"

* * * *

Luckily the Tupperware had held and Mary Beth was able to heat up the spaghetti she'd made without having to scrub Eli's floor first. As she heated the sauce up in a pot, Eli came behind her and wrapped his arms around her stomach. With his head resting comfortably on her shoulder Mary Beth had never felt so comfortable in her own skin. Or Eli's T-shirt and shorts. They were a matching pair of lovers. His shirt was big on her, but not really long enough to not need shorts of some sort.

"That smells good," he cooed in her ear as he kissed her neck. "Almost as good as you."

"We need to eat, so stop that before you end up bending me over the table and I burn dinner."

At the mere mention of sex Eli hardened behind her.

"What am I going to do with you?" she chided as she stirred the sauce.

"I like your last idea."

"So did I actually," Mary Beth confessed and used her butt to push Eli back. "Now scoot and set the table."

"Fine," he grumbled like a petulant child. "If you're going to force me to."

"Yes, yes I am."

As they sat down to dinner, Eli told of growing up toward the end of the family line verses Mary Beth's position as first on the list.

"Funny, I got away with much more than Carlos or Angelica ever did because they paved the way, I guess. After some of the stuff they pulled my parents decided I wasn't so bad."

"I doubt you were bad."

"I wasn't really, I'd learned what to avoid because of their mistakes too."

"Then I guess my sister Jillian won't get pregnant at seventeen."

"Probably not. Not that it was a bad thing you did. I mean look at Luke, he's a pretty good kid."

"Not really. At least he didn't get that from me."

"Why do you always put yourself down as a mother?" Eli asked as he set his fork down. "You make little, off handed comments all the time about how if it wasn't for this person or that person your son would be licking the windows on the short bus."

"Because it's true. I don't know what I'm doing as a mother."

"Most first time moms don't. My sister was lost with Gloria, then David came along and you'd think she was born to be a mother."

"Please, I can see the judgment in other moms' eyes. They constantly look at my son like he's one second from juvie."

"I doubt it. He's a good kid."

"I know it just…" Mary Beth pushed an Italian sausage around her plate.

"Why aren't you a good mother, Mary Beth?" Eli asked as he set down his fork and scooted closer. "Luke can read and write at age five. He clears dishes and loves you more than anything in the world. He's respectful to adults. Where's the bad seed smoking *Luckies* behind the dumpster."

A weight sat heavily in Mary Beth's chest as acid burned its way up her throat. Luke was a good kid, but she couldn't see her hand in forming him. She was the one who half the time heated up a meal to make sure he at least had food in his belly before his bath.

"Who taught him to walk?"

"We all did."

"Who was the first person he got up and walked to?"

"Me." Mary Beth swallowed the lump in her throat as she remembered his first toddling steps.

"What was his first word?"

"That's up for debate. Maury swears it was Maury, but Gabbie says it was Mommy."

"I think Gabbie's right. When he runs a fever and his belly aches who does he want?"

"He's fine with any of the girls or Maury."

"But who does he want?"

Mary Beth crossed her arms and turned her head away. Eli placed his hand on her chin and turned her back to him.

"Tell me something, do you let him snuggle in next to you in bed when he's scared or sick."

"Of course."

"Does he tell you about his day at school or just say nothing?"

"He's a motor mouth after school."

"You're who he loves and wants approval from. You're his shelter and the one person above all he knows will protect him. You're a good mom. Quit trying to be perfect because there isn't a perfect mom in the world."

"My mom is."

"If she was she would have been there for you when you got pregnant to council you through any decision you made. She wouldn't have chastised you for not making the choices she made growing up."

"I was wrong."

"Yeah, but Luke's one of those mistakes that ends up being a good thing. Like when the chocolate fell into the peanut butter jar."

"Why do you try to make me think I'm not an utter failure?"

"Because you're not. I don't know who's in your head telling you that you are, but I want to have a long, possibly violent, discussion with that person."

Eli had fury in his eyes and as usual Mary Beth couldn't help feeling it was directed at her.

"Maybe I should go. I'm upsetting you—"

"No, you're not. Even if you were, that's okay. Normal people have disagreements. What makes you think you always have to make me smile?"

"Isn't that what a...what did you call me?"

93

"*Mi reina?*"

"Yeah, that. Isn't that what a *mi reina* should do?"

Eli sat back and gave her a sly smile.

"Your mother never fought with your father did she? You never heard them through the walls fighting?"

"No."

"Your mother had a lot of built up rage. I'm sorry she took it out on you."

"No she didn't."

"Any woman who has a husband cheating on her as regularly as your father has rage."

Well, she had to give him that.

"She didn't just take it out on me. Mandy...even as a child, could tell she wasn't wanted. I tried to over compensate, but you know when you're not wanted. When she was younger she rarely came to my house and by the time we all had cars...it's sad because right now she's the only sister I can talk to."

"Aren't you two talking?"

"No...maybe...I don't know. Like I said we weren't the best of friends to begin with. If it wasn't for Gabbie, I think she'd have gone to college and forgotten about all of us. Gabbie, Sarah, and I are kind of the core of our group. Mandy skirts it. Then again, with Gabbie, Sarah skirts it. It's weird."

"You all came together in a crisis."

"That we did," Mary Beth said with an upturned smile. "But didn't I promise you a drama free night?"

"Not that I remember, you just said I wouldn't get a show. Kind of missing it."

"I'm not. I like being with you, Marquez."

"You're not so bad yourself, Wallace." Eli got up and cleared their plates. "Hmm...you said something about spending the night didn't you?"

"I had to get you to let me in."

"So it was a ruse?"

"Maybe, maybe not."

Eli took her hands in his, pulled her up, and walked the two of them to his old, brown, plaid couch. Mary Beth had seen this pattern in many basements over the years. She wasn't about to judge the hand-me-downs, especially since the only reason she didn't have the same in her apartment was because she no longer had someone to hand to her.

"We need to talk about something," Eli's tone was ominous.

"Okay." Mary Beth forced a second lump from her throat.

"I was serious in my bedroom."

"About?"

"I need you to be mine. I don't share. Especially my women."

"How many women do you have?" Mary Beth growled.

"Right now? None."

The sharp tone smacked Mary Beth.

"Oh, do you ever have more than one?"

"If there was more than one how could I ever call a woman mine?"

Good point.

"I'm not Nate, and I sure as hell am not your father."

"What makes my father worse than Nate?"

"Carrie knows about Luke, other than that, not a thing. I want to give you my heart, Mary Beth, but I'm not about to give you an inch more than I did in that room if you can't do the same."

"I'm not in love with Nate. I was raised to believe the father of your children should be in your life forever."

"In your life doesn't mean he has to be a part of it."

Eli brushed back a stray hair from Mary Beth's forehead, and then cradled her face in his hand.

"I want you to be *mi reina.*"

Tears pricked the sides of Mary Beth's eyes. Elias wasn't using his accent to send her hormones into a frenzy and cloud her thoughts. He was laying it all out to her. His rules weren't there to hurt her like Nate's.

Nate had wanted her to be available for him as he needed her. Even before she got pregnant, their dates were at his convenience. She placated herself with the idea he was focused on improving his game so he could make it big and they'd be together forever. He couldn't see her because he was in the weight room or at the batting cages, even though he never was. Nate had been so attentive to her, until she slept with him.

Then he'd come by or have free time enough for maybe dinner or a movie always followed by sex. How had she mistaken that for love? Because he might hold her hand on the way to a class or two? Idiot.

No, not an idiot, a fool. She wasn't going to be fooled twice. Then she looked into Eli's obsidian eyes and remembered his words.

"You want to be a nun until marriage I'd still love to eat what you brought me, but don't bottle up your feelings or put on some damn fake persona you think I want. Mary Beth, the only thing I want from you, is you."

"I love you, Elias." Her voice didn't tremble, wobble, or even catch. As she said the words, she felt something she'd never felt in her life—light. There was no longer a weight on her shoulders. Her head that ached every day released and a dizzying euphoria came over her.

Eli brought his lips to her and laid her back on the couch.

"I'll make you one promise," he said as his hand pressed against her juncture and she felt the tingling heat spread up her body. "If I ever make you cry I'll spend every second of my life making it up to you, *mi reina.*"

Chapter Eight

Healing yourself is connected with healing others.
—Yoko Ono

"All right ladies, it's time to make a really big decision," Gabbie said as she, Mary Beth, Mandy, and Sarah sat together in Mary Beth's office in mid-October.

The center had the last kid picked up, minus Luke, Claire, and Charlie who were spending the extra time in the Children's House room with Case. It was time for the owners of Growing Strong to make some big decisions. Up until now, Gabbie and Mary Beth had been crunching numbers, looking at projections, and getting a feel for at least their current client's feelings about a move.

"Mary Beth has found a few grants we'd be eligible for and started writing up proposals for them, but before we submit we need to know what you guys think."

"About what?" Mandy asked. "I thought we determined a few years ago we wanted a school? Or were we just going to sell this place after we're all trained in and go to different schools?"

Mary Beth had never thought of the latter until Mandy said something. Her best friends could scatter to the wind. She was the only one not in the Montessori training program. She could end up as sole owner of this day care center, forever. What would she do without her friends by her side every day? Her daily headache tightened like a vice over her left eye.

"Mary Beth." Gabbie snapped her fingers in front of Mary Beth's face. "Out of your head."

"I'm sorry, what did I miss?"

"Nothing. We saw you zone," Sarah said as she popped a few chips in her mouth. "Quit scaring her, Mandy. You know she takes everything you say seriously."

"Who says I'm not serious?" Mandy asked as she turned her head to the side. "I have the ability to be serious."

"Why would we break up?" Mary Beth asked, knowing full well why Mandy was pulling away. She'd been pulling away since the championship game. "The reason we're successful is because we can count on each other. If I didn't have you guys I'd be on every assistance program known to man trying to hold a job that pays two bucks over minimum wage. I know I probably haven't said it enough, but every one of you means the world to me."

"Awe, thanks," Mandy sneered with a glare that tore through Mary Beth. "I'm so glad we could be here to help you out."

"Knock it off, Mandy," Gabbie snapped.

"Whatever." Mandy stood. "Decide what you want. Whatever works for Mary Beth, you know we'll all just follow along to help the poor princess so she can succeed. I've got somewhere to be."

Mandy stormed out of the building, leaving the other three to try to figure out what the hell was going on.

"What was that?" Sarah asked.

"Should I go after her?" Mary Beth looked at Gabbie whose lips were a straight line.

"No, I'll talk to her later. She's not really..." Gabbie cocked her head to the side and scratched at her hairline. "The thing with your...her dad is making her relive a lot of painful things. You don't know how it was between your mother and her. You know how it is to hear your mother's voice in your head...Mandy's never felt comfortable anywhere. Even with her mom. She always had to stick up for her because no one else would. Now she can't justify why her mother did what she did. She actually feels sorry for your mother, which of course has her caught in a paradox she can't reconcile."

Mandy had been ignoring Mary Beth for a while now, but that was just a normal Tuesday, nothing strange. She should have reached out to her, but the thought never crossed her mind. They were both hurting. They could have been each other's crutch through this time. Instead, much like Mandy pointed out, it was all about the princess and what she needed.

"There was always another baby." Isn't that what her father said?

"Let's talk business while Mandy cools off. I'll run everything by her once I've calmed her down," Gabbie insisted.

"You sure?" Sarah asked.

"Yes, we've put this off for too long." Gabbie sighed and pulled out the surveys. "As you know we've surveyed our families and found that about sixty-four percent would love to have us continue their children's education. The negative part is most of their kids are under the age of three. Which means—"

Sarah interjected. "We'd have to wait for two years to even begin to have a full school and then—"

"And then who knows if they'd still feel the same way," Mary Beth said. "God knows when it was time to sign Luke up for school I lost all my excitement for the grade school I went to as a kid. After a few years of you guys teaching him I couldn't imagine them doing anything with him."

"We have that in our favor at least." Sarah smiled.

"Realistically the grants I've found could provide us with the funds to bridge the gap. One is a five-year renewable resource that would help with the purchase of a building and all of those costs."

"With the building covered," Gabbie began. "Couldn't we pay the wages out of the daycare income?"

"Yes, we could, and if we stay at the current capacity minus the building fees and maintenance we could afford one to two more staff."

"The other thing we found on the surveys was a suggestion to have an information night. To discuss the different education methods."

"We'll need more than one," Sarah replied. "One for our parents, then two or three for prospective parents."

"She's right," Mary Beth said. "Sarah, would you mind working with me on that? You're almost done with the training at least for the elementary level."

"Not a problem. Did you guys ask on the surveys about before and after school care?"

"No, what do you mean, Sarah?" Gabbie asked.

"Right now we have two dozen kids that get picked up and dropped off by the school bus. Just because a parent doesn't choose to have their kid in our school doesn't mean we can't still provide the same service they enjoy from us now."

"We were thinking about keeping the same hours, at least in the beginning," Mary Beth said to Gabbie. "Even having both an infant and toddler room for a few years as feeders to the Children's House program."

"What would that do as far as the state is concerned? Would we still be labeled as a school or daycare?"

"If the sections are separate, we may have to find a facility with multiple entrances, possibly a second LLC…it's all just paperwork."

"Your favorite thing in the world," Sarah mocked.

"I live to serve." Mary Beth smiled. "But if it funded the school for the first few years, it could be a good idea. It would also make it so the Montessori trained staff we have now could just work school aged kids. The infant and toddler room can be staffed by people with just early childhood certification."

"What about magnet status, so we wouldn't have tuition? We're talking working class people—even a small fee is going to be a strain."

"Should we move to your neighborhood, Gabbie?"

"Then we'd lose all of our kids. I don't want to start from scratch and Woodbury isn't as rich as you think."

"Um, don't you have to go through a gate to get to your house?" Sarah asked with a cocked head.

"No, you don't, that's two neighborhoods over."

"You should have known—she lives there, they let any riff-raff in," Mary Beth said, and then dodged Gabbie's toss of a stress ball.

"Back to the topic at hand, since unlike you two I have a life," Sarah teased. "Where is the mysterious building?"

"Elias' brother Carlos is a realtor and Elias said he'd be happy to find us some to look at."

"Neighbor boy has all sorts of connections." Sarah's eyebrow rose. "And what else does he provide?"

"Loans, backrubs, and bedtime stories, if I'm lucky."

"Bedtime stories?"

"He's been tucking Luke in lately so I can work on Gabbie's goal to take over the world through the Montessori method. Mwahahaha."

"Is he just tucking in Luke?"

"You know we're dating…did I not share the info?"

"Mary Beth talking about personal things?" Sarah looked up in the air like she was trying to remember the last time that happened. "I remember a date she didn't return from until the A of the M, but for all I know she played Canasta all night."

"Canadian rules. Four decks are more fun. Now you know, I'm meeting the family at his grandmother's birthday this weekend. So, yeah, you're caught up. Mandy's not here so no need to go into the other details."

"We enjoy other details too," Gabbie said as she leaned her elbows on her knees.

"Okay, you tell me how many orgasms Case gave you the last time you were together and we'll compare notes."

"More than Eli, every time," Case broke into the conversation and the room heated up with red-faced women. "Are you guys done with *business* talk?"

"We were discussing the loan process—" Mary Beth tried to explain, only to get Case's hand held up.

"I don't get loaned out," Case said as he crossed his arms. "And neither does Gabbie, so when you're done discussing sex like this is a football locker room, can I please have my wife back?"

"We really weren't discussing…" Gabbie got the same *I'm-not-about-to-hear-it* hand. "Right, okay, so you're the money woman, if the loan looks good with a nice rate I say we go forward."

"Only if we get the grants," Mary Beth added. "If we get the grants I'll start looking for buildings."

"Look for them anyway," Case interjected.

"What?" Gabbie asked surprised.

"Look for them anyway, you guys will make it work. If not, you'll take out a few kneecaps. You could probably certify this spot as a school in a pinch. If you need help…well, my dad's old firm specializes in criminal defense, but they could still look over the contracts and legalese you need. Gratis."

101

"Thanks, Case," Mary Beth said.

"You know I love you all." He winked. "And it was somewhere in the range of five or six."

"What was…oh," Sarah began. "Well hello Mrs. Thomas and how was your coffee this morning."

Case walked out of the office and Gabbie buried her face in her hands. Sarah and Mary Beth burst into laughter.

"And on that note," Gabbie said, "I'm going to leave."

"If you can still walk," Sarah called after Gabbie who held her middle finger up behind her back in case Charlie and Claire came out.

Sarah sat back in her chair and eyed Mary Beth.

"What? That was a good meeting right?"

"Meeting the family."

"Yes." Mary Beth gathered her papers and tapped them a few times on the desk to even them out. "You're all caught up."

"You really like him."

"Yes, I do, I…love him." The words caught in her throat. This real love thing was harder than she thought.

"Love. Like Nate love?"

"Like grown up love. That is, if I can figure it out."

Luke rushed into the office and jumped on Mary Beth's lap. She was beginning to think she'd have to tell him to stop doing that soon. He was getting big. Instead, she enjoyed that he still wanted to do it in the first place.

"We ready to go."

"We are."

"You coming, Auntie Sarah?" Luke asked. "We're getting pizza."

"Pizza," Sarah said wide-eyed and over excited for Luke. "Extra cheese."

"Yep."

"So cheesy I can tie you up in mozzarella?"

"Yep."

"You're lucky your mom and I have more work to do. You're just going to have to eat your way out of pizza jail tonight, mister."

* * * *

The smell of pumpkin spice filled Mary Beth's apartment even though her bars were completely cooled. As she frosted them with cream cheese frosting, a knock on her door sent a buzz of nerves down her spine.

It'd been three weeks with Eli, and to top it off, Nate hadn't bugged her once. Normally Luke would have been moping around and depressed. Instead, for the first time ever, he hadn't noticed his absent father.

"Are you ready, *mi reina*?" Eli asked as he swept her up into his arms. She giggled— actually giggled—as she wrapped her arms around his neck.

"Almost, I have a little bit left to cover."

"I think you're too covered already," he teased and tried to raise her navy blue sweater.

"Stop it." She smacked his hand. "Luke is just finishing tying his shoes in his room. He could walk in here any second."

"So?" Eli said as he pressed her body against the island and kissed her so deeply she felt it in her toes. "All he'll see is his mother smiling for a change."

With a light brush of his thumb along her bottom lip he claimed her as his while his tongue swept against hers. A creamy coffee taste heightened the sensation when he cradled her head in his hands. Mary Beth's fingers tangled in his thick, dark hair and she became lost. Eli's body pressed firmly against hers and his knee slid between her thighs and pressed up.

"Oh God," she moaned into his mouth as he gently rubbed his thigh against her center. The fabric caused a friction that made her fear she wouldn't stop. "Please do that again when Luke's asleep tonight," she begged as she clung to his hair and moved her mouth to his ear.

"Anything, *mi reina*."

One of these days she was going to have to ask what that really meant, but right now the inflection in his voice told her everything she needed to know.

"Yes, *oso chiquito*."

Eli grimaced at her even though she was sure she'd gotten the pronunciation right, but then he smiled and kissed her on the nose.

103

"Hey, Eli," Luke called and they broke from their embrace.

"Hey, Lucas Maximus, you ready to meet my crazy family?"

The phone rang and Mary Beth sighed. It was Nate. Did that man have radar to tell him when she was happy?

"Hello."

"Hey, Mary Beth, you're going to be there by four, right?"

"Be where by four?"

"The bowling alley. My whole family's going to be there and they expect to see Luke."

"You didn't say anything about a bowling alley."

"Of course I did."

"No, you didn't. We have plans today."

"Since when?"

"Luke and I do a lot of things on Sundays."

"My parents and grandparents will be there. You know, the only grandparents Lukey has."

This was when she hated Nate the most. Eli looked up at her as he inspected Luke's shoe and gave him a high five for doing a good job. How could she explain to Eli she couldn't go with him? But Luke only got to see his grandparents on special occasions and even then it was fleeting.

"Could you pick him up?"

"Mary Beth, everyone wants to see you too."

"Who's everyone?"

"My mom, Nana June, and you know Luke only behaves when you're there. Plus, a job came up so I won't be there." Mary Beth turned her back to the guys and went into the kitchen.

"Why today?"

"I don't know. Nana and Pop-Pop came down to the cities for some reason."

"How long are they going to be bowling?" Mary Beth pinched the bridge of her nose.

"Who knows, it could go to nine."

"I was supposed to go with Eli today. Can you please send our apologies?"

"You're keeping my child from his grandparents now? Because of some random guy you're sleeping with."

"No, but can't your mom take him?"

"Mary Beth, if you don't have my son at the bowling alley by four thirty—"

"Fine. I'll bring him."

"Good and you better stay too or—"

Mary Beth hung up and wiped her eyes when she felt Eli's warm hands on her shoulders.

"You okay, Mary Beth?"

"Nate's family is having some gathering and I have to bring Luke."

"Can you still come to my *abuela's* party?"

"No, Nate has to work so he needs me to take Luke."

"What about people there? Can't he just be with them?"

"No," Mary Beth snapped. "I'm sorry, it's not you, it's Nate and his stupid, last minute...I'm sorry, I'm not mad at you, just the situation. His grandparents will be there and he's their only grandchild." Mary Beth turned, wrapped her arms around Eli, and buried her face in his chest.

His hand stroked her hair and he kissed her head.

"Don't worry about me. It's not a big deal. Take Luke where he needs to be. I'll see you tomorrow." Eli's face scrunched up for a second, then released. His eyes betrayed the small smile on his lips.

"I'm sorry."

"Don't, it wasn't your fault. Trust me, I know who I'm mad at."

"The same person as me?"

"It better be or we'll need to have a serious conversation."

"No conversation needed."

Eli kissed her forehead and headed to the door. "Have fun with your nana, Luke."

"Nana June?" Luke asked as he went to Mary Beth. "Nana June's part of Eli's crazy family."

"Nope, just yours. We're going to have to skip seeing the crazy Marquezes so we can see the even crazier Schmitz family."

Eli held Mary Beth's hands for a second and she could read the disappointment in his eyes.

She mouthed the words *I'm so sorry*, but he just shook his head.

"Too late," Eli said and headed for the door. "I see where I stand."

"That's not fair."

"The whole situation isn't fair. You don't have boundaries with him and he'll always come first."

She wanted to tell him it wasn't Nate she was choosing over him—it was Luke, but he was already gone.

"Damn it." Mary Beth could feel the swear words and hatred building inside her. She wanted to yell at Luke because he was the reason she couldn't go with Eli, a man who cared what she wanted. Who wanted her to be happy and comfortable. A man who turned her on because her pleasure was more important than his. It wasn't Luke's fault either, it was… "Damn it, Nate, I hate you so much."

"What, Mama?" Luke had heard her even though she'd said it under her breath.

"Nothing, Lukey, just Mama really wanted to go with Eli today."

"Cuz you love him and not Daddy?"

Mary Beth kneeled down and placed her hands on Luke's shoulders.

"I'll always love your daddy because he gave me the most amazing kid in the world." She just didn't like the jackass, she thought to herself.

"You don't love Eli?"

"I can love more than one person at a time."

"Kinda like Daddy loves you and Carrie."

Bile rose in her throat and burned as she tried to swallow away the taste.

"It's different than that."

"If you marry Eli will Carrie love him like you love Daddy?"

"No." This was getting more complicated as Luke got older. Nate should have just married her in high school.

As soon as the thought entered her mind, she felt shame overcome her.

Why was she such a damn crybaby at times? No, not at times, at shit that dealt with Nate. She had been crying in Gabbie's office last spring and half the summer. The sad part was, she knew she didn't even love Nate and hadn't for years. He was just who she knew and no matter how much she wanted to ignore his calls, she couldn't. Not while being a good mother to Luke.

Chapter Nine

If you cannot get rid of the family skeleton, may as well make it dance.
—George Bernard Shaw

At the local bowling alley Mary Beth pushed into the darkness and walked the lanes looking for the Schmitzes. The alley was packed. She kept Luke tight to her body even though he was having one of his, "I'm big and don't need to hold my mom's hand," moments. Yeah right he behaves better with me, she thought.

On lane twenty-three she saw Nate's mom. Her high, blonde hair had been teased in the same style since the late seventies according to the family pictures at Nate's house. Mary Beth laughed thinking high school had to be Mrs. Schmitz's hay day.

Suddenly Mary Beth stopped in her tracks. Her father was joking with a few of his buddies at lane nineteen.

With a much clearer head and no rage she noticed gray had settled in along his temples, and laugh lines marked the sides of his eyes. His athletic build had only firmed since she'd left home and she knew he took pride in his hours spent in the gym. Now she wondered if it was the hours spent or the women he met that drew him to the gym.

Suddenly the laughter stopped and he turned around to see what his friends already saw. Luke tugged on Mary Beth's arm, trying to get to Grandma Schmitz four lanes down.

"Mama, come on," he whined, but Mary Beth couldn't move.

Her father stared at Luke. Why wouldn't he just talk to her? What would it kill him to engage his daughter in conversation? Oh yeah, she blew up at him last time and he knew he still owed her an explanation.

"Mama, Nana and Pop-Pop." With another strong tug Mary Beth lurched forward and her father turned in shame.

When they got to lane twenty-three, Nora was doing a dance after picking up a spare.

"Well, what are you doing here?" she sang and came over to collect a hug from Luke.

"Nate said there was a family gathering today that we had to come to."

"Why would he say that?"

"Where's Nana June?" Luke asked.

"Nana and Pop-Pop are getting ready to go south, Lukey."

"Daddy said Nana and Pop-Pop would be here!" he pouted.

"Well, Grandpa Schmitz is coming over with a pizza now so how about you go with him so I can talk to Mama."

Luke went up to sit at the table behind the lane with Nate's dad. Nora took Mary Beth by both hands and sat her down.

"What's going on? You look really upset. Is something bothering you?"

"You tell me. Nate said I had to come here today or else."

"Or else what? Honey, he can't threaten you. I love my son, but if it weren't for you, Luke would be covered in dirt and starving. This is league play so we're always here on Sundays. Today's nothing special."

"Nothing special. Damn him," she cursed under her breath. "He figured it out."

"Figured what out, sweetheart?"

"I've been seeing someone. Today is his grandmother's birthday party."

"Can you still make it?"

"It started at three." Mary Beth's phone buzzed and Nora snatched it from her. When she checked the number she winked at Mary Beth.

"Nathan Lucas Schmitz, what kind of crap are you pulling?" After four years of Nate living in her basement while the mother of his child not only created a home for herself and Luke, but also started her own business, Nora had come to respect Mary Beth. "I don't want your excuses. You made your choice years ago. If it doesn't involve you seeing Luke leave her alone…it was great to see him, but I didn't need to…I'm done…love you too, goodbye."

"Thank you," Mary Beth said, taking her phone back.

"Even if all you do is clean up, go to the party. Don't let Nate trap you. Lord knows I never let his real father do that to me."

"Wait…I thought…"

"There's a reason Nate's the way he is. I thought a stable guy might stabilize him—obviously I was wrong. Genes—who knew? Then again, I wasn't like you were when he was little either. He doesn't remember his real dad, heck I doubt if his real father remembers he had a son and that's okay." She looked lovingly up to her husband. "George has been there every step of the way, even when I was slipping he didn't let Nate fall. You find yourself a George, just don't cut us out completely. I love that little boy more than you know. He's my second chance." She turned to Mary Beth. "With you as his mom he'll be a good boy."

Mary Beth felt tears pricking the corners of her eyes. She couldn't believe her ears. Nora was saying she was a good parent? Amazing.

"Enough of this crap, or you're gonna throw my game off." She turned and faced Luke. "Luke, you wanna go to the party you were supposed to go to?"

"The crazy Marquez family?"

"They're crazy?" Nora growled.

"No, Eli was just being silly with Luke."

"Yes, go have fun with the crazy ones."

Mary Beth thrust her arms around Nora and squeezed. "Thank you…thank you so much."

"Hey, some days I think the only thing Nate did right was to have Luke with you," she said as she patted her head. "I love my boy to pieces, but I need to teach him his bullying gene came from me."

* * * *

Eli entered the Wellstone Center and headed for the room they'd rented for the day. Inside, his mom and aunts were hanging the last of the decorations and dressing tables. His sister and cousins were stirring dishes and setting out plates for the buffet.

"Hey, Eli," Carlos called. "Where's Mary Beth?"

"I don't want to talk about it," Eli grumbled and crossed to a table to sit down.

"Wait a minute, you're telling me that this girl you were bringing to meet grandma isn't here? Man that has to suck."

"It's your deeply sympathetic demeanor that has always seen me through."

"Awe man, come on. You've never brought a girl. I thought you'd finally grown up."

If by grown up Carlos meant finally feeling the sting of rejection, then, oh yeah, he'd grown up in spades. He wanted so badly to share this experience with Mary Beth. He wanted her to at least have met his *abuela* and for his *abuela* to know he'd found a good girl. Even with a child out of wedlock Mary Beth was a good, Catholic girl. She'd only lapsed in her faith because of the twisted interpretation her mother had forced on her. Mary Beth would be welcomed with open arms at any parish.

"You know me, man, I'll never grow-up," Eli teased, hoping the pain in his voice didn't resonate. "Is the bar open yet?"

"Ever since the men arrived." Carlos slapped Eli on his back and led him to the coolers of liquor in the corner.

It was about five or six beers later, Eli wasn't sure because the empties in front of him were starting to fuzz together, when he turned and saw a red head talking to his sister. She was tall and looked like she feared for her life as she held a pan of some baked good. Eli assumed she must be lost. He turned back to the empties in front of him and wondered if he'd need a half dozen more before the pain stopped.

"I was wrong," a soft voice said behind him. If he didn't have such a profound buzz going on he would have sworn it was Mary Beth. "Did you hear me? I said I was wrong, Elias. You were right."

"Excuse me," he said as he turned toward the voice from the two headed she beast behind him. No wait…once his head stopped spinning the two heads became one.

"I said I was wrong. I should have come here with you from the start."

"Is that *mi reina*? No, *mi reina* does not love me. She'd never choose me over her ex-asshole that treats her like shit."

In his mind this sounded strong and forceful, but to those around it was a drunken bluster of half English half Spanish wobbling from his mouth.

"Let's get him some coffee," his sister said as she and Eddie got him up and walked him to the corner.

"No." Eli wrenched himself away from the two of them—only to have the world go all kattywompus on him and spin in a way his center of balance couldn't recover from. Falling forward, he landed on Mary Beth who had tears in her eyes as she cradled his head to her chest and guided him to the floor.

"I'm so sorry."

"You said that already, when you chose him over me."

Mary Beth brushed his hair back from his eyes and smiled at him.

"The last thing I'd ever want to do is hurt you. I see I have. And I'd never want to hurt the man I love."

"If you loved me you'd have come here first."

"I'm new at the real stuff. I only know the childish crap that Nate said was love. Give me a little bit of time."

"No, I want you to never talk to him again," he pouted.

"That I can't do, though I wish I could."

"It's because of him isn't it?"

"Nate, no, Luke, yes."

"He likes me better you know."

"Luke? Only because he's over playing with David and doesn't see you sprawled out drunk on the floor."

That began to sober Eli as he took in his surroundings. His sister returned with a warm cup of coffee and a glare.

"You fucking idiot." She spoke in Spanish. "How could you do this at grandma's party? Because of some *güera*? You better marry her if she turns you this stupid."

"She's *mi reina*."

The little crowd that had surrounded them all looked as if he'd smacked them in the face.

"*Mi reina*? *Mi reina*? You did not just call her that?" Eddie snapped at him.

"It appears my grandson has made his choice," the old crackled voice of his *abuela* cut through the crowd. "And like most Marquez men he's acting like a damn fool because of his queen."

Eli looked at Mary Beth who would not have understood any of the last few minutes of conversation. Yes, to call a woman *mi reina* was reserved for those to whom you are married, but for Eli, Mary Beth was who he wanted forever. She was his queen and would be forever if he could sober up enough to explain himself to her.

"So," Eli said, sobering slightly from the caffeine. "You want a beer."

"No," Mary Beth replied and kissed his forehead. "You've had enough for both of us."

"Yes," his grandmother's English always had a heavy, thick accent and most had problems understanding it. He hoped Mary Beth wouldn't be one of them. "I am Elias' *abuela*."

"It's an honor to meet you. Happy birthday," Mary Beth said as she shook her hand, only to be wrapped up in the patented grandma hug and receive the kiss blessing.

"And you, are you to take my Elias."

"Take him?"

"I think she means accept and love him," Angelica said.

Mary Beth's face flashed red.

"Um…yes…I guess."

"No, guess. Just yes or no. Never guess."

"Then yes."

"That's a good girl." Eli's grandmother's soft wrinkled hand patted Mary Beth's. "Come, we talk, Elias' queen."

Oh shit, Eli's secret was out, and not just to his family.

"I can help clean up. It's the least I could do coming in late and probably adding to Eli's current state."

"Elias, clean? What a smart idea. I like your queen, dear boy."

* * * *

"She didn't say clean," Angelica whispered in Mary Beth's ear. "She said queen. Elias declared you *mi reina*, his queen. Men only declare their wives *mi reina*."

Mary Beth felt the blood rush from her head, causing the dizzying feeling she hadn't felt since she told Elias she loved him.

"He just told me that it meant I was his." The words came out as little more than a croak.

"He wasn't lying."

"His queen?" Mary Beth looked at Eli whose eyes were wide like he'd just been caught with his hand in the cookie jar after his mother had told him no.

Queen. Queen. The word bounced around Mary Beth's head as she and Eli's eyes stayed locked on each other. His family revealing this secret had sobered him quickly. A queen was revered. Worshiped even. There was only one queen to one king.

A spark lit inside Mary Beth, the spark Elias always talked about between them. The room disappeared as she saw only him at the end of a very long tunnel. He was only three steps away, still sitting on the floor, but the space between them caused an ache in her heart. She needed to touch him and feel his arms around her. She needed to have him cradle her and keep her safe. She needed to taste his lips and run her fingers through his thick black hair. It wasn't the sex, although he'd shown her more than a few levels of pleasure over the last few weeks, it was the love, the worship he showed her. She was his one and only. More importantly, his queen.

Cutting the space between him and her, she captured his lips. It was strange to taste the hops from his beer, but it didn't matter, he'd sobered now and was meeting her excitement with his own. She sat sideways on his lap as he wrapped his arms around her. He was right—when they got together they stoked the fire between them and never squelched it. They may have to learn how to someday, but today, right now, she wanted to make sure he was the only man on her mind. He was who she wanted.

"Your queen, huh," she said breathlessly when they finally broke from their embrace.

"If I knew this was the way you'd react I would have translated sooner."

"I'm glad you didn't. Coming from Angelica it made it more meaningful. You boys don't know how to describe important things."

"You do know you have a pretty large audience right now."

"It's starting to hit me."

"Latino and red head…dangerous combo."

"I'm learning that."

"And now I'm on the clean-up crew. I'm teaching you Spanish so you don't get confused again."

"You sure you want to do that?" Mary Beth's lips became full and ached remembering how sexy it was to have him whisper unknown words in her ears.

"I'm not letting my sister translate some of the things I've been saying to you."

Mary Beth lost her breath at that. "Are they still looking at us?"

"Oh, yeah, we're better than the Super Bowl."

"Is Luke still distracted by David?"

Eli looked over her shoulder then back to her.

"It appears so. You're not going to be too embarrassed to go with my grandmother are you? She seems to be waiting for us to unhook to take you somewhere."

"Should I be afraid?" Mary Beth whispered with a smirk.

"Petrified. I'm her favorite grandson."

"Are you now?"

"What can I say, the ladies love me."

Mary Beth arched her eyebrow at him.

"But I only love one lady." He kissed her softly on her lips and they both got up off the floor.

"Good, now, come," his grandmother said more forcefully as she shuffled to a table on the other side of the room. "You need to pull magnets apart sometimes."

At least that's what Mary Beth thought she said.

The discussion between her and Eli's grandmother lasted over an hour between the language barrier and the fact Eli must be her favorite because she grilled Mary Beth on everything from her past, present, and future. Even though his grandmother was a little, old, wrinkled lady who'd made it to her seventies and talked softly, she scared the crap out of Mary Beth. She must have trained the FBI's interrogation team.

Eli came by when he'd finished cleaning up and rescued her. Saying a few loving words in Spanish to his grandmother, she smiled and patted

Mary Beth's arm before Eli's father curled his arm around her elbow and led her out of the hall.

"Does she like me? Or hate me? I can't tell."

"Really." Eli smiled. "Guess you'll have to learn Spanish to find out."

"Oh that's not right, *oso chiquito*."

Eli shivered at her perfect pronunciation of his nickname.

"After how you reacted when you learned two little words I'm afraid to teach you more."

"Are you sure, oso—"

"Who told you?" Eli interjected.

"Me? Who would tell me anything?" Mary Beth said innocently.

"I hate that nickname."

"Why? You are a little teddy bear."

"Does that mean I get to be snuggled in your arms all night?"

Luke ran up with David.

"Mama can David sleep over?"

"It's a school night, Lukey."

"Oh, yeah, I forgot, I guess not, David."

"It's okay, my mama would say the same thing."

"Tell me about it," Eli grumbled and Mary Beth flicked him.

"But can he come to my party?" Luke's eyes lit up.

"Party?" Eli asked. "You're having a party without me?"

"No, yous gonna come with my mom." Luke's forehead knitted together in worry. "Weren't you?"

"It would have been nice if you asked me. I can do things without your mom you know."

"Oh, well, will you come to my party and bring David?"

"What's it for?" Eli asked as if it would actually determine his attendance.

"My birthday. I'm turning six."

"A sixth birthday party." Eli scrunched up his face and rocked back on his heels.

"At the water park."

"Water park?" Eli's eyes lit up like David's did.

"Really, with slides and everything?" David blurted.

115

"We'd love to come to your party as long as we get cake," Eli teased. "When is it?"

"I don't know," Luke said as he tugged David. "Come on let's find your mom."

"It's in a few weeks at the Water Park of America."

"I'm not missing the prince's party, as long as it's not going to be an issue with Nate that is."

Mary Beth wasn't even sure if Nate would show up. She'd told him about it and initially he said yes, but not showing up at the last minute was his specialty.

"The prince seems to think of you and me as a matched pair." Mary Beth wrapped her arms around Eli's neck. "And I love that he thinks of you as an extension of me. He's never had that."

"I told you I'd never hurt you or Luke."

"I'm sorry about what I did today."

"It's forgotten."

"You know it wasn't about Nate, right?"

"I figured that out. Especially after Angelica and I talked while I cleaned up. You want Nate in Luke's life."

"I was always told a father should be in his children's lives. It was the most important relationship."

"Not if the father isn't one."

"I'm learning that, but I need Luke to make that choice and as long as he wants to be with his dad and his dad's family, I have to make him available."

"That's okay," Eli kissed her lips, then trailed kisses to her ear and whispered. "But you're not part of the package."

Chapter Ten

"No one can make you feel inferior without your consent."
—Eleanor Roosevelt

Mary Beth steeled herself as she looked at her childhood home. At the edge of Oakdale, the split-level home only differed from the rest on the block by its cobalt blue siding. Hedges created a gate of green around the front and side of the house. Mary Beth hadn't dared step foot on the front stoop she'd spent so many years sitting on as a child.

She saw herself at ten with her stupid pigtails eating a bomb pop they'd gotten from a passing ice cream truck. Her brother, Wills, ate an ice cream sandwich next to her. Even though her mother had abandoned her when she needed her most, Mary Beth couldn't do the same.

A bus stopped at the edge of the block and she saw a group of high school aged kids get off. Two red heads that looked familiar began walking toward her home. It couldn't be? Little Jillian had only been eight the last time she saw her. But there she was, her shoulder length, strawberry blonde hair pulled back by two barrettes on either side of her head. She wore a gray hoodie, jeans, and a pair of sheepskin boots. Mary Beth searched for the round-faced child who cried when she hugged her goodbye, but she was a young lady now.

Carrington, Carry, her brother, must be a senior now and looked every inch a grown man. At least six-five with the strong, but lean, build of a football player like their father. His hair had always been the darkest of the Wallace kids, still with a tinge of red, but now it was dark auburn.

Mary Beth didn't even realize she'd gotten out of her car until her siblings stopped dead in their tracks. She was a pariah, the one they were not to engage in conversation with for fear of the same treatment. As much as she wanted to wrap her arms around the children she'd helped raise, she didn't want to hurt them either.

"What are you doing here?" Carry asked. He eyed the house as if he were scared.

"Who cares?" Jillian said as she sprinted to Mary Beth and wrapped her arms around her.

Warm tears fell from Mary Beth's eyes as she held Jillian tightly.

"I've missed you so much you little monkey."

"No one has called me that since you left."

Mary Beth pulled back from the embrace and smiled at her.

"Did you stop climbing trees?"

"No, although I'm too tall for gymnastics now."

"Well, duh, I tried to warn you," Mary Beth chided her sister who was almost as tall as she was now.

"Jill, we need to get inside. Mary Beth, I'm glad you're doing good and all, but—"

"I'm here to see mom."

"She won't see you." Carry's eyes turned down in shame.

"Even with the divorce?"

"What divorce?" Jillian asked. "They're not getting a divorce. Dad's taking her to St. Thomas and they're renewing their vows in a few months."

"What?"

"Over New Years. We're all going."

"Jillian, Carry, in the house, now," Mary Beth's mother's sharp tone cut through the air like a knife.

"Sorry, Mary Beth," Jillian said with a shrug.

Carry patted her shoulder as he walked by. "I don't know what you heard, but they've never been happier."

"Mary Beth, you're not welcome here," her mother snapped as she crossed her arms. Her red hair was pulled up in a tight bun and she wore a tan turtleneck sweater and long jean skirt.

"You're still doing it."

"Doing what? Protecting my children from negative influences. Yes. I'll do that till the day I die."

"I saw him you know. Dad. With Ariel."

"I don't know what you're talking about."

"Funny, who's the bride going to be at New Years, because I'm hearing different stories?"

Her mother stiffened as she crossed the yard to confront her.

"If I've heard about it, I'm sure others have too. I just came here because I thought you might need support, even from the fallen whore."

Her mother turned her head to the side and swallowed hard. When her lips pulled in Mary Beth saw a side to her mother she had never seen before. Hurt.

"I guess he thinks I'm not strong enough to survive."

"He said you'd be fine and that Jillian was in high school and he's raised her the best he could."

Her mother turned back to Mary Beth and shook her head.

"You're not a little girl anymore. It's hard for me to adapt. Wills is in college still, graduate studies, but with him in college he still seems like my baby."

Mary Beth wanted to tell her mom she was in college too, and she could be her baby still. Instead, she chose silence, because there was something unnerving in her mother's placid tone.

"I wasn't talking about a divorce." Her mother crossed her arms tight around her body. "I've got cancer. The kids don't know about it. I should tell them because the chemo's getting harder for me to handle. There's no reason for young minds to fear things they can't control."

The piercing, emerald eyes that had comforted Mary Beth through sickness and heartbreaks were now pooling with tears. The eyes that pushed for homework to be done and for Mary Beth to clean her room. The ones she'd never seen ever waiver now looked defeated.

"It's one thing for Kevin to stay with that woman all these years… he could have at least helped me through this instead of buying me a tombstone. I suppose you're happy?"

"Why would I be happy to hear you're sick?"

"Dying. Right? So he can remarry your best friend's mother."

"My sister's mother you mean."

"He did tell you everything didn't he?" Her mother let out a long breath of air.

"No, he didn't tell me about you being sick and that...I made a scene."

"Why would you make a fool of yourself?"

"Funny, I thought the same thing about you when I heard."

"It's not foolish to be with the father of your children. You'd know that if..." She waved her hand as if the action could make her mind be clear of her negative comments.

"For years I believed that. Not anymore. I stayed with Nate. Not dating him, just sleeping with him in hopes he'd marry me so you'd accept Luke and I. I became the other woman when he got married. All because I needed your approval, but you live in a fantasy world where your husband's remarrying you and pledging to love you forever when he never loved you in the first place."

"Your father loves me. He loves the home I've created. I'm a good wife and mother to him. I'm Fai—" the word caught in her mother's throat causing her to gasp for air.

"Faithful? Is that what you wanted to say? You've been cheated out of a good man for years. You could have had a man that loved just you. Instead you stayed and pumped out kids for him. Why? To keep him?"

"I got married before God." Her mother placed her hand on her chest. "I promised forever."

"You didn't break your vow, Mom, he did. You didn't fail, he did."

"He's your father." Her mom's bottom lip quivered as the first tear Mary Beth had ever seen fell from her mother's left eye. "You respect him."

All these years her strong mother was as petrified as Mary Beth had been. Afraid to upset a man who already had one foot out the door. No wonder she had been so hard on Mary Beth growing up—one small argument could have been used as an excuse to leave. If he left, then she would have been the failure.

Mary Beth wrapped her arms around her mother. She knew better than to expect a return hug, but she had to let her mother know she was loved.

"Mom, he failed you. You are a wonderful wife and a pretty decent mother."

"Not wonderful?"

"You kicked me out..." she said as she stepped back. "And I still say you were decent."

"I was so scared he'd blame me if I didn't take a stand."

"I bet you a million dollars if you actually served him with the divorce papers you should have twenty–five years ago he wouldn't know what to do. I'm just glad I learned it six years in with Nate and not twenty. Why would Dad have to do better for you? You give him everything he wants and never ask for more. You or Ariel. I feel sorry for both of you. But unlike you, I'm done being scared of what people think and I'll be there for you if you need me."

Mary Beth walked back to her car and opened the door.

"Wait. I have some of your things still in the house. Can you stay for a little bit?"

Mary Beth looked at her watch.

"I have to pick up my son by five so I have a little time."

Mary Beth closed her car door and stepped onto the property she was told never to darken with her presence. In the front window Jillian and Carry watched as their mother put her arm around Mary Beth and leaned on her for support.

* * * *

"It was amazing, Eli," Mary Beth gushed as they did the dishes and Luke worked on his pluses at the table. "She apologized and told me everything. Not in front of Jillian and Carry of course, can't let herself waiver from the Iron Lady too much, but...I don't know."

"What do you think happened when your father came home?"

"Beats me. She said she'd come to Luke's birthday party. Isn't that great. Jillian and Carry too. Wills and Gwen are both away at college. She's so proud of them."

"Did you tell her about all you've been doing?"

"A few classes at a junior college, no I didn't go into detail about that."

"Why not? You're doing great and your business is about to take off."

"Right," she scoffed.

"Crap, she's back."

"Who's back?"

"Doubting Mary Beth. She's so not sexy."

"What?"

"I like the confident Mary Beth. She's so damn hot. I'd do anything for her. This Mary Beth, well she still has the legs, but I doubt she'd know what to do with them. Let alone me."

"Is that a challenge?"

"Is that the pitcher that broke her catcher's hand?"

"I didn't break it, recently at least."

Eli slid in behind Mary Beth and nuzzled against the crook in her neck.

"*Mi reina, eres la mujer más sexy que conozco.*"

Mary Beth exhaled a ragged breath and Eli could only imagine what she'd do if she knew what he'd said.

"That is so not fair."

"I have to use what I've got."

"I don't care if you're reading me a loan contract. If you do it in Spanish with that voice…"

"Oh…*mi reina*, can I please tuck you in after Luke's asleep?"

"Only if you help me with stats first."

"You kill me, woman. Fine, but you don't need help."

"Okay, how about you just crack the whip and make me finish my homework instead of distracting me."

"Deal."

"Momma," Luke called from the table. "All done."

"Okay, I'll come check it."

Mary Beth went and sat at the table, praising Luke for every correct answer and helping him with ones that weren't. She never scolded, just refreshed him on a lesson he'd been taught at day care. Eli wondered how he could be so lucky as he saw her smile and tease Luke, who was having as much fun working with Mary Beth at the same time.

It'd taken her a while to relax around Eli, but when she did she became the most beautiful woman in the world to him. Damn, he'd really fallen in love, hadn't he? Oh yeah, long legs, beautiful eyes, and the heart of a mother. Ugh, his brothers were right, he was a teddy bear.

He didn't want to be taken care of like a child, but whenever he thought of the woman he'd eventually marry, he always pictured his parents' relationship. The way his mother loved his father and how she took care of the whole house. She was loving, sweet, loyal to a fault, and protective as anything. There was no sneaking in late at his house, not because of the punishment, but because his mother was always up waiting with a cup of tea pretending she got caught up in a movie and didn't notice the time.

"You're not fooling anyone, Mom," he'd tease as she offered to warm up leftovers for him.

"Me," she'd say, innocently, *"I was just letting your father get fully asleep because I snore like a bear."*

"No, you don't, but I love you anyway."

"So, did you have a good time tonight?"

"Yes, Mama."

"Good. You won't need extra confession time tomorrow will you?"

"That depends." He sighed as he spooned some leftover rice into his mouth. *"Is it okay to have murderous thoughts about your brothers or is that a sin too?"*

"You boys." She smiled and her slippered feet padded their way back to her bedroom.

"Nigh-nigh, Eli," Luke said, tugging on his pant pocket and taking him from the memories.

"Night, Lucas Maximus." Eli picked him up and gave him a big hug as Luke gave him a kiss on the cheek.

"Four days till my birthday party."

"I know, big man, it's circled on my calendar."

"No skippin'."

"I wouldn't miss it even if kidnappers took me an hour before it started to New York and tied me to the Statue of Liberty."

"But how would you get back in time?"

"I'd run."

"You're not that fast," Luke said and giggled as Eli placed him back on the floor.

"Not normally, but for your birthday party I could beat The Flash."

"Sweet."

123

"Now, get to bed, because you'll need all the rest you can get this week to make it up ten floors to the big slide."

"Ten floors?" Luke's eyes got big.

"That's why we're going to the Water Park of America isn't it? To go on the big slide."

"I don't know."

"But I need you to keep me from being scared on it."

"We can go down together?"

"Duh!" Eli ruffled Luke's blond hair. "I'm not going down that thing on my own."

"All right, daredevils, it's time for bed," Mary Beth said with her hand outstretched for Luke.

Eli instantly got hard at the idea. Mary Beth must have caught on by the glint in her eyes when she saw the reaction.

"I have homework remember."

"I didn't do anything."

With all the dishes dried, Eli plopped down on the couch and waited until Mary Beth came out of Luke's room.

"Why does he keep checking with me about his party?"

"Nate makes a lot of promises to him about going somewhere or doing something. This is the first time he hasn't had me calling to check with his dad every day to make sure he's still coming. Eli, I know this is still really new, you and me that is, but I'm getting uneasy about how Luke is with you."

Shit. They'd known each other for less than two months. Of course she was nervous.

"I never thought about dating a guy and how that would affect Luke. I should have learned after Nate and all his girlfriends that I didn't want to do that to Luke. Then again, I didn't think I'd meet anyone that made me forget about his father, let alone one that was so accessible."

"You want me to be less available?"

"I meant because you're two doors down. He ran to your door when he got scared. I'm very happy you were there and that he feels so comfortable with you…"

"I'm not looking for short term, Mary Beth." She looked as caught off guard as Eli felt saying it, but it came from his heart. "And I'd never do anything to hurt Luke. I love these dinners and for the first time in my life, I want more than a few nights with a girl. I know it's hard for you to do, but tell me what you want and I'll do it."

"I don't want to hurt my son, but I don't want to stay with a man to protect Luke either."

Eli's chest tightened and his stomach knotted.

"What are you saying?" The words came out scratched and pained through Eli's swollen throat.

"I'm saying right now you make me happier than I've been in years. If something happens, I need you to be strong enough to make me let you go. I held on to the idea of Nate well past me loving him all because of Luke."

"How am I supposed to know when you stop liking me and are just playing for Luke?"

"I never said dating me would be easy."

Eli slowly regained the ability to breathe and his racing heart began to return to normal.

"Let me get something straight, you're not kicking me to the curb right now."

"Oh, God no," Mary Beth said as she covered her face. "That's what it sounded like, didn't it?"

"Uh, yeah."

"I'm not good at this."

"I gotcha. At least you know how to get my heart racing."

"Your heart raced?"

"I didn't say that," Eli lied as Mary Beth crossed to him and straddled his hips.

"I'm pretty sure you did."

"Well…damn it, woman…I…I…I love you, okay? I don't want to go anywhere and even if you hate me, I'll still love you and I won't let you go. So there."

"You really are the baby of the family, aren't you?"

"Second youngest, thank you very much miss oldest who thinks she must be obeyed."

"Oh, I must be obeyed at all times."

As she leaned in to kiss him, Eli fought every urge to take possession of her lips and ravish her right then and there. Turning his head to the side she slowly kissed her way up to his ear.

"Why did you turn away from me?"

"Because you have homework and I will not let you use me like a piece of meat and get distracted from your work."

"I'm going to be distracted thinking about how good you feel inside me while I work if you don't take me now," she whispered in his ear, sending electrical charges from his neck straight to his groin.

"Good, then you'll be wet and ready when I do."

She let out a trembling breath and pushed off the couch.

"I'm going to hurt you tonight when I finish my homework."

"Need me to go buy some zip ties?"

"What makes you think I don't already own some?"

As she sauntered to the table and took out her book, Eli's cock strained against his pants and no amount of shifting was going to lessen the want. She was going to tear him apart when she finished her work. Oh yeah, she was the woman he was going to marry someday. He knew that so deep in his soul it scared him.

Chapter Eleven

All the art of living lies in a fine mingling of letting go and holding on.
—Havelock Ellis

"You have everything?" Eli smiled at Mary Beth who had three armfuls of supplies. "Isn't the point of having the party at a water park is that they take care of everything?"

"We're spending the night in the hotel and..." She looked on both of her shoulders and at the small luggage bag she was pulling. "I'm over doing it aren't I?"

"Just a little? What's Nate bringing?"

"Himself, maybe a present for Luke."

"Maybe? Is he helping you pay for the party?"

"He didn't have the funds right now."

"So you're paying for him?"

"And Carrie and his parents. I did the birthday deal so really I'm paying for everyone. That's what parents do."

"Yes, parents, plural. Not my place. I'll back off."

"Thank you, I'm stressed enough as it is."

Mary Beth could already feel her headache working its way up from the back of her neck and wrapping around her skull.

"I have a cure for that?"

"I don't have time for your cure-all."

"I'm there for you if you need me. You know, ten minutes, sneak back to your room for a—"

"Hi Eli," Luke said, breaking up Eli's devious thoughts.

"Told you I'd come to your party. I don't break promises to someone as important as you."

Luke beamed and Mary Beth blushed.

"Can I help you carry the stuff to your car at least?"

"Yes, please."

After loading the car Eli headed toward his.

"Aren't you riding with us?" Luke asked.

"You're spending the night at the hotel remember," Eli said.

"So?"

"So how am I going to get home after the party if I ride with you?"

"There are video games in the hotel room, I thought we were gonna play? Momma said I could stay up late since I'm six now."

"But you're still going to bed at some point."

"There are bunk beds, you can take the top," Luke reasoned.

"Really? I can have the top bunk?" Eli's enthusiasm made Mary Beth turn her head to the side.

"Sure, Momma didn't want me to sleep on that one anyway."

"What if I'm too tall to sleep there?"

"Then sleep with Momma."

It was so simple in Luke's world.

"Honey," Mary Beth finally stepped in on the conversation. "Eli can't sleep in my bed. We're not married. It's not appropriate."

"But he did before."

"No he hasn't." Mary Beth was adamant.

"Uh huh, I seen him."

"When did you see Eli in my bed?"

"I had a nigh'mare and he was there."

"Oh yeah," Eli said, and held his hands up as Mary Beth raised her eyebrow at him. "I forgot to tell you…"

"You forgot what?" Her face was red as hell and he loved it.

"I kinda fell asleep and um, left after Luke came into the room."

Mary Beth covered her face with her hand and tried to control herself.

"Luke, Eli was helping Mommy with a problem from school and we both must have fallen asleep. Eli doesn't sleep in Mommy's bed normally."

"Oh, but can he have the top bunk?" Luke asked not missing a beat, obviously not caring about sleeping arrangements outside of this evening.

"Yeah, Mary Beth, can I have the top bunk?" Eli asked as he moved in closer to her. "I really want the top bunk."

"I hate you both right now," she whispered and let her lip curl up.

"Long-term, *mi reina*," Eli said, solemnly.

"Get in the car."

Luke cheered and Mary Beth hung her head in defeat.

For the first time since Luke had been born Mary Beth hoped Nate bailed on them. She wanted the party to just be Eli and her hosting. That was so wrong. Nate was Luke's father and no matter how much she hated him at times she couldn't let Luke lose that part of his life.

After checking in, Eli made a show of climbing in the top bunk to make sure he fit.

"That was sweet of you to go on the top bunk."

"I'm sleeping up there, I don't know what you're thinking."

"You're going to squeeze onto a twin mattress."

"Jealous? I know you wish you could have the top bunk."

Mary Beth laughed at Eli as he ran ahead to catch up to Luke and put him on his shoulders.

"See now you're big enough for all the rides."

After they checked in, Mary Beth felt nervous as she waited on the other families to show up. Slowly the mafia arrived as well as David and Gloria with their mother.

"Thank you so much for letting them come," Angelica said. "Can I give you some money to help cover their admission?"

"No, it's fine. Luke wanted David to come for sure. They've been playing together quite a bit in the pool lately as it is."

"That's great. So, you and my brother?"

"What about us?"

"Tomorrow, come to our parent's house for supper. You won't want to move after a day at the water park as it is. Let us cook for you."

"Oh, meeting the parents…" as she said it Nate came in with Carrie.

"Daddy." Luke sprinted to him and they had an exchange.

"Okay, sounds good. If you're sure I wouldn't be intruding."

"Are you crazy? Please, my mama is dying to meet you since she didn't get a chance at the last party."

After grandma's interrogation Mary Beth wasn't sure she could handle another member of Eli's family drilling her.

"Why?"

"Oops," Angelica said as she checked her watch. "I've gotta run."

As Angelica took off to the parking lot Mary Beth turned to Eli.

"I forgot about your niece and nephew."

"I'll pay for them."

"Not that. When you got in my car. They're supposed to be at your apartment tonight."

"Darn it, I didn't think of that either," Eli said with a slow slick tone that let Mary Beth know he hadn't forgotten his responsibilities. "Guess I have to give up the top bunk, huh?"

"You little shit."

"I told you I want long-term." He leaned in and kissed her on the cheek.

"Auntie Befs, we goin'?" Claire asked as she tugged Mary Beth's hand, pulling her from the heat of Eli's personal space.

"Yes, sweetie, how about I get you guys your bands and you can get started."

Mary Beth got bands on all the people present and told them to meet at the tree house for food at one o'clock. Nate straggled behind with Luke.

"Can you take Luke in and get him started?" Mary Beth asked Eli. "I'll be in soon."

"What's with you and the neighbor?" Nate asked once Eli had gone inside. "Why is he here?"

"Because Luke asked him and his niece and nephew to come."

"Then why were you making out with him?"

Mary Beth's throat went dry as her gut ceased in on itself. She had the right to kiss any man she wanted to. Nate was not going to ruin this for her.

"That explains why I never understood about decent kissing. If you think a guy kissing me on the cheek equals making out, maybe you and Carrie need to watch more porn together."

"What's that supposed to mean?"

"I saw the videos when I was in your room. Listen, I don't want to talk about it. I need to wait for your parents and a few other guests."

"My parents aren't coming. Maybe you should have considered the fact that they probably wouldn't want to go down waterslides for four hours when you planned their *only* grandson's birthday party. You're so selfish sometimes, Mary Beth."

"Hey, back off." Eli had been waiting by the door instead of heading straight in when he stepped into the conversation.

"I can handle this," Mary Beth said as she put her hand up.

"This is for Luke's parents to discuss, not a guy who's trying to screw his mother," Nate warned.

"If you want to dictate the terms of your son's party, why don't you be a man and pay for it."

Nate wrenched Mary Beth's arm as he pulled her away from Eli.

"Don't put your hands on her." Eli's stern tone was new to Mary Beth, and as much as she didn't want to be turned on by his valor, she was. He freed her arm from Nate's grasp and held her tightly to his body.

"This doesn't concern you." Nate stuck out his chest and squared his shoulders to Eli. "And Mary Beth you know I pay my due when it comes to Luke. How dare you lie like that about me?"

"Lie? I didn't lie and I didn't just blurt out the fact I was paying for everything. I'll be more than happy to have you go over there and pay the balance before we go in."

Nate glared at her as his nostrils flared.

"Daddy, stop," Luke pleaded, and Mary Beth's heart broke for him.

"Nate, Luke needs to go inside. Why don't you and Carrie take him and you can cool off in the water?"

"Why don't we just take him?" Nate snapped.

"What?" Mary Beth's chest tightened.

"You heard me. I'm not really liking our arrangement when it comes to him."

"The one where I have him ninety-nine percent of the time and you get him when it's convenient for you?"

"I'm a little more stable then you right now. I don't have random women coming in and out of the house."

131

"You're delusional." Mary Beth pulled Nate into a corner so Luke didn't hear her. "If it wasn't Luke's birthday and it wouldn't crush him, I'd kick you out. Don't ever threaten to take my son from me."

"Our son. He's half mine."

"Only when you're not busy or bored and want a playmate. It's an empty threat. I'm allowed to see other guys. Having Luke around never stopped you from dating."

"You're his mother. He already isn't going to respect you because we're not together and everyone knows that's your fault, not mine."

The headache that had just been a dull pounding from nerves got worse behind Mary Beth's right eye, and she lost vision. Bracing herself against the wall she held back the vomit creeping up her throat.

"Get the hell away from my sister." Mandy's harsh tone cut through the lobby of the park.

Mary Beth kept her head down, but could see Nate hadn't moved.

"Don't start with me, Mandy."

"How 'bout I finish you? Take Luke inside, be a dad, and play with him. Or did you forget this day was to celebrate how awesome of a kid he is. It's about him, not you. Leave her alone. You can fight with her three-hundred-and-sixty-four days a year. Not this one. This one is Luke's."

"We're not done," Nate growled in Mary Beth's ear as he took off to take Luke into the park.

"Eli, come on," Luke said. "You promised the big slide."

"I'm coming," Eli replied. "You got her?" Mary Beth heard him ask in a low tone.

"Always," Mandy replied.

Mandy's warm hand began massaging Mary Beth's tensed neck muscles.

"Is it a bad one?"

"Really bad." Mary Beth swallowed the acid burning up her throat.

"These migraines are completely stress related. You know that."

"Yeah, I know. I'm just trying to keep my breakfast down and regain sight in my right eye."

132

"I heard someone was castrated as they went down one of the slides." Mandy's way of saying things with authority always made Mary Beth smile.

"They were not." Mary Beth stifled a laugh.

"I'm sure I could find a way to make it happen today."

"That would just lead to a big settlement for him."

"You ruin all my fun."

"I'm a mom." Mary Beth's stomach was settling a little as she placed her hand on her belly. "It's my job."

"Eli went with Luke, right?" Mary Beth asked as she slowly opened her throbbing right eye to check her vision.

"Yes."

"Good. Nate's threatening to take him because I'm dating Eli."

"It's official then?"

"Yes. Has been for a few weeks now. Nate caught Eli kissing my cheek and accused me of making out in the lobby."

"Nate thinks every woman should be his. Let's get some fresh air in you and see if that helps."

Mary Beth finally lifted her head and took in her friend. Mandy's eyes were blood shot, but she still had the same caring eyes she only showed in private. "You okay?"

"Allergies, nothing big."

Mary Beth tried to smell if Mandy was hung over, but the chlorine in the lobby was irritating her already throbbing head.

"Oh great," Mary Beth groaned, feeling the full bag on her arm. "Luke doesn't have his floaties."

"It's okay, I'm sure Nate...well, Elias won't let him get hurt."

"If Nate will let him near Luke."

Mary Beth waited on a bench for the stragglers. After ten minutes, she was ready to go in. Her migraine had lessened to a dull headache brought on from the stress of planning the party that she wanted to be perfect and she knew she could live with that ache. It was stranger to not have it.

"Who are you still waiting for?"

"My mom said she'd come with Carry and Jillian."

"Your mom?"

"I didn't tell you, we talked." Mary Beth scanned Mandy's face to make sure she was okay with the choice to invite her family. "I went by the house a few days ago."

"How's she doing?"

"Dying of cancer, at least that's what my dad thinks. She's sure she'll beat it."

"Your dad's divorcing her because she's sick?"

"They're not getting divorced. At least they weren't when I talked to her."

"Let me get this straight. Your...sorry, *our* dad is telling my mother he's getting divorced and they'll finally be married. When in truth..."

"He's hedging his bets." Mary Beth's lips pursed in disgust.

"That's..."

"Nauseating. If she lives, then he 'can't leave her' because she just survived cancer."

"How were we raised by such weak women?" Mandy asked as she leaned against the wall.

"Have you talked to your mom?"

"A few times. She says she doesn't need to explain herself to me."

"What about Dad?"

"Not yet. Mom says he wants to sit down and explain himself, just not right now."

"Convenient."

"I thought so."

"Mandy, I know it's been hard on you, but I am your sister and coming here today proved how strong a bond we already had."

"I wasn't missing the demon spawn's birthday for anything." She smiled. "You know I didn't mean it...what I said in the office. I should have apologized a while ago. It's just..."

"You don't have to tell me. There a thousand apologies I owe to people, but I'm too afraid to say them."

Mary Beth grasped Mandy's hand and leaned her head on her shoulder.

"I'm so damn glad you're my sister. That should have been the first thing I said when I told you. After the nausea that came with the thought of our parents together, that was one of my first thoughts. You stuck by me even after everything my family put you through."

"You've got a pretty selective memory there, Wallace."

"Do I?"

"Yeah," Mandy said, as she patted Mary Beth's head. "Because I clearly remember more than once you standing up for me and telling your mother to take a flying leap."

"I never said that."

"Yeah, you did. Remember when she wanted you to stay home and help her with laundry instead of coming to my birthday party? You told her you'd do it all by yourself the next day if she'd just let you go. When she went off about me being a slut and a dozen other things you told her to take a flying leap and that she didn't own you. 'The second I can move out of this house I will and I'm moving in with Mandy when we go to college. We'll become lesbian lovers and drink all night till we flunk out or end up as sex slaves in the Middle East.' Your mother's face was priceless."

"That's because she actually believed you'd let me do it."

"I kinda wished we could have been roommates because you made it sound fun. Travel, sex, maybe a few days on the Mediterranean, then see the great pyramids."

"Hello Mary Beth, Amanda." Speak of the Devil. Mary Beth's mother made them both jump.

"Damn, she still makes me nervous," Mandy whispered in Mary Beth's ear.

The feeling was mutual.

"Hi Mom, I'm glad you could make it."

"Do they have a discount if I'm just going to sit? I wouldn't want you wasting money on me." Her mother was prim and proper as always with her hair in a tight bun and herself in a perfectly tailored camel's hair car coat.

"I'll ask."

Jillian rushed Mary Beth and Mandy with teenage glee and strong hugs.

"Please say everyone is here," she blurted.

"Gabbie and Sarah are inside already. You'll have to meet Gabbie's kids. They are adorable."

"Gabbie's a mother," she balked.

"She adopted her husband's siblings…it's a long story. But Claire and Charlie will keep you in stitches."

"What about your kid?"

"Luke, he's inside with Nate."

"You're still with Nate?"

"No, I'm not." Mary Beth swallowed hard. "But it is Luke's birthday."

"A boy. I didn't know you had a boy. I imagined a cute little niece."

"You have an adorable nephew. He will not disappoint, I promise."

"Gabbie's got two kids," her mother chided. "Amanda where are your three?"

"Back off." A surge of acid shot up Mary Beth's throat, and it was then she realized she said that, not Mandy. "You don't know anything about my friends or me. They've been there for every birthday, cold, first step, and laugh. If you can't act like an adult, you don't need to meet your grandson. He's done just fine without you until now."

The chill that tore through her mother was visible to the group that was staring at her. Jillian looked as if they'd just shot her puppy, Carry had the strong disapproving eyes her father wore, and Mandy's shoulders were squared instead of sunken in. Mary Beth reached for her hand and squeezed. Her mother looked from one person to another and her stiff face relaxed.

"I'm the last person to be casting down judgment on you or Amanda. I apologize. Glass houses, rocks and all." She turned toward Mandy. "Thank you for being there for Mary Beth and Luke when I could not."

After changing into their swimsuits, Mary Beth, Mandy, and Jillian entered the water park. Carry came out of the men's locker room and wrapped his arm around her. She marveled at the kid who was now a half a foot taller than her. He was always the cuddliest of the family and she loved that he hadn't changed. Eli walked up to her with a look of concern until he eyed Carry and she saw the jealous side of him emerge again.

"I've missed you, queen bee," Carry said as he squeezed her tight.

"I blocked out that name," she laughed.

"Mary Beth, I think you need to go to Luke," Eli said.

Mary Beth feared her mother's glaring eyes at her with every decision she would make with Luke today. *"Why would you put a yellow shirt on him? You know he'll just get it dirty and you don't know how to do laundry properly."* If Luke threw a tantrum, or even said no to her, especially in public, it would brand her as a bad mother.

"I have his floaties. Is he freaking out?"

"Not about floaties."

Mary Beth ground her teeth and felt the sharp pain returning to her temple.

"Where is he?"

"The FlowRider."

"He's not tall enough for the…"

"You okay?" Jillian asked.

"Yes, just another reason to not have a child out of wedlock."

"Mary Beth," her mother said as she took her hand. "No more of those comments. I've been thinking since your visit that it was wrong of me to judge you."

Mary Beth steadied herself as she waited for the 'but', only it never came.

"Thank you," Mary Beth said, still unsure of the context.

As they walked around the corner, she saw Luke standing on the side keeping a steady face as Nate rode on the simulated surf ride. Sitting on his knees on a boogie board he rode up and down on the hard rushing water. When she got to Luke he looked as if he was on the verge of tears. She knelt down and brushed Luke's still dry hair to the side.

"I can't believe you haven't taken Eli on the slide yet."

Luke turned his head confused by the statement. If nothing else Mary Beth had gotten really good at redirecting Luke's focus.

"He came over to me pouting about not getting on the slide yet."

"You did?" he asked Eli over her shoulder.

"Duh, I came here to play with my best friend and he takes off and won't even splash me."

Luke smiled and Eli extended his hand to him. Mary Beth introduced Luke to Jillian and Carry as they all walked up to the top of the ten-story family slide. All five of them rode back down in the blue and yellow inflatable tube. Luke clung to Eli the whole ride down and when they got off Mary Beth finally introduced Luke to his grandmother.

"What do I call you?" he asked.

"What do you want to call me?" her mother asked.

"I call my other nana, Nana June. Then there's Grandma Schmitz. Are you a nana or a grandma?"

"My name is Grace. I'll let you decide if I should be Nana or Grandma?"

"Okay, Nana Grace. Do I have another Pop-Pop too?"

"Pop-Pop Kevin. He couldn't come today."

"Oh, that's okay. My daddy can't come to stuff sometimes."

Mary Beth's mother grasped her hand and gave Mary Beth a knowing squeeze.

It was over an hour before Mary Beth saw Nate again, and she had to track him down when she went to find him.

"It's time for food and presents," she said as she found him snuggling on an inner tube with Carrie on the lazy river.

"Where have you been? I was worried about Luke. He just disappeared."

"I can see how freaked out you were."

"If he would have been taken I know you would have locked down the waterpark and hotel. Maybe all of Bloomington."

"Would you get out of the water and come upstairs for the party?"

"Fine." Nate and Carrie pulled themselves from the water and followed her upstairs. "Is that your mother?"

"Yeah, Jillian and Carrington too."

"Man they got big." Suddenly Nate's tone got harsh. "I thought I said your fuck buddy needed to leave."

"Nate, that fuck buddy has been playing all day with your son. Eli's not going to leave."

"You marrying him?"

"It's too early for that discussion, but he's who I want to be with."

"What about us?"

"What us? There hasn't been an us in years."

"No, you and I haven't been together for a few months…" Nate pulled her to the edge of the room. "I've been miserable without you. You know you're the only one—"

"Stop. There's nothing you can say that I'll believe or care about anymore. You gave me a wonderful son, but, Nate, we need to limit interactions to being about Luke. He's who matters."

"What's that supposed to mean?"

"It means I want a custody agreement."

"Why?"

"Maybe it's so you can't just threaten to take my son when you get a burr up your ass. Or maybe, just maybe, it's so Luke can know when he gets to see his dad instead of 'oh surprise, Dad's here for three hours'."

"This is about Eli, isn't it?"

"This is about Luke." Mary Beth's hand flew between the two of them. "Just Luke, not me, not you, him. He needs you in his life and I'm willing to work with you, but if you don't care then you'll need to sign away your rights completely."

Chapter Twelve

Being deeply loved by someone gives you strength, while loving someone deeply gives you courage.

—Lao Tzu

Snow had covered everything overnight. As Mary Beth, Luke, and Eli sat in Carlos' car, they listened to the plan for the day. Eli's brother had promised to help find a new home for Growing Strong.

"I've got five properties that I think could work. One had been a school and now the district's trying to get rid of the building. It's the most expensive, but would need the least amount of renovation."

The first two buildings were little more than warehouses that had offices. Mary Beth nixed them immediately. When they pulled up to the third property, Mary Beth felt tingling down her spine. It was in a residential neighborhood and right across the street from a park and lake. Although it was a single story building, it took up over half the block. Only two houses remained on the far side of the parking lot. Unlike traditional buildings, this one was round in shape and had small slit windows that Mary Beth was already imagining busting open to let the sunshine in.

"Now this had been an elementary school. It closed just a year ago. Built in nineteen seventy-three, the building is in great shape. There's a little graffiti on the far side of the building, but no damage inside. Twenty-six rooms are already set up as classrooms, some bigger for the music and art programs."

As they entered the building Mary Beth could hear children's laughter as they went from one classroom to the next. Eli's brother went on about how there had been a head start program in the school for preschoolers. Between that and the three kindergarten rooms they wouldn't have to lower the cupboards and bookshelves. Everything was already at eye level for the kids just like Gabbie said it needed to be.

"It has room for us to grow," she said with a nervous sigh. "That's for sure."

"What grades will your school encompass?" Carlos asked.

"Initially we hope to have a Children's House level to third grade. Eventually moving to sixth. I'm not sure if we'd go to junior high or not."

"Momma, could this be your office?" Luke asked, as they entered the school's central command center in the middle of the building.

"Maybe that one," she said as she pointed to a smaller corner office that currently had *Assistant Principal* stenciled on it.

"Why not the Principal?" Eli asked.

"Because I'm not going to school for that. Gabbie is. I'm going to school to crunch numbers."

"Let's head to the cafeteria, then the gym." Carlos led them down the hallway.

"What's that?" Mary Beth asked, pointing to the yellow stain on the ceiling.

"The district did say that the building needs a new roof. We could write in your loan docs up to half the cost of a new one."

"A new roof on a house costs twenty grand," Mary Beth groaned. "I can only imagine what one here would cost. Even with the district eating half the costs."

"Please," Carlos chided. "You're practically married to a Mexican. Give him a half hour you can have twenty guys fixing your roof for nothing."

"Excuse my brother," Eli said as he punched Carlos in the shoulder. "He's ignorant sometimes."

"There are good stereotypes and bad ones. You gotta lighten up, *oso chiquito,* if you want to be with a *güera.*"

"All joking aside…" Eli held Mary Beth's hand. "What do you think of the building?"

"I love it, but I need to get some estimates on the roof as well as take stock of your connections."

"Oh, so now you're going to joke about the migrant workers."

"You know what they say, if you can't afford 'em, sleep with 'em." Mary Beth winked at Eli and took off across the gym with Eli hot on her tail.

"You think you can trade sexual favors for day labor, huh?" he teased when he caught her by the waist and swung her around.

"I did get a great deal on a car." She laughed, practically choking.

"Oh yeah." He pinned her hands above her head on the wall as he used his body weight to hold her hips still. "You planning on taking care of every guy on the roofing crew?"

"I don't know, are they as hot as you?"

"They would be my relatives." Eli smiled and Mary Beth warmed.

"You might want to keep me tied up in your bedroom then. You know how Marquez men get me going."

"Do they now?" he asked as he took possession of her throbbing lips as if she were the last woman on Earth.

"Excuse me," Carlos said. "But Luke is here and you're supposed to christen your first home, not your business."

"Sorry." An embarrassed Mary Beth tried to regain her composure.

"Momma." Luke came up next to her. "They have basketball hoops here just like at my school."

"I see that."

"If I wents to school here who be my teacher?"

"If you go to school here," Mary Beth corrected. "Probably Sarah."

"Really?"

"Yes, she'd have a co-teacher, I'm just not sure who'd that be right now."

"That'd be so cool."

"Carlos, I think this is the spot. If your brother would unglue himself from me let's take some pictures and can you get me some specs?"

"No problem."

"Are you sure you want me unglued?" Eli growled with his accent on full as he raised an eyebrow.

"Right now, yes, but if the deal goes through I have a feeling you'll be helping me late into the night cleaning this place up."

"Now the migrants have to be on the cleaning crew."

"Only because I want to do a thorough check of your paperwork." Mary Beth let her eyes tell him everything she wanted to do.

"Eli has homework?" Luke asked.

"Yeah, and can you believe he colored a door green instead of blue."

"A door is a rectangle, Eli," Luke scoffed.

"That's it, Luke, you're my new teacher."

* * * *

By December Luke had become a regular at Jessica and Petey's on Tuesdays. At first Mary Beth had been nervous about him overstaying his welcome, but every Monday Jessica would call Mary Beth to make sure she could pick up Luke after school the next day.

Usually Mary Beth would come up with an excuse to leave after five minutes of small talk, but today she wanted to talk longer. Jessica had offered more than once to be someone she could lean on when it came to Nate. Whether Mary Beth wanted to share or not, Luke did. Jessica was easy to talk to and with her social work training she'd had an easy demeanor that Luke was drawn to.

Jessica looked amazing as always when she opened the front door and greeted Mary Beth.

"Hello, Mary Beth." She smiled. "Let me get Luke."

"Jess, can we let him play for a few more minutes? Maybe have a cup of coffee?"

"Is something wrong?"

"No, but in the past you've offered to help me if I needed it."

"It's nothing serious is it?"

"Nothing bad, let's put it that way."

They went into Jessica's kitchen. She had an island in the middle with a black tiled surface. Cabinets and appliances wrapped around the island of the rectangular kitchen with a window on one end over the sink and a dining area on the other end.

"Sit." She offered a seat at the island as she poured two cups of coffee. "Cream, sugar?"

"Cream please," Mary Beth said as she let the warm cup heat up her cold fingers, more from nerves then the winter season baring down on the city.

"So, what's going on?"

"I need to know how to set legal parameters with Nate. We never had any before because we never stopped being together. I thought it was what I was supposed to do. He is Luke's dad and I never want him to not know him."

"Luke talks to me a lot when he's here. Who's Eli?"

"Eli's my boyfriend. I've never had one before. Is the relationship upsetting Luke?"

"No, in fact if he didn't call him by his first name and I didn't know about Nate, I'd think he was his dad."

"Really?"

"Yes, he talks about Eli like Pete talks about his father, Blake. What do you want for Luke and Nate?"

"I want Luke to have a relationship with his father. I don't say negative things to him, even though I could, because I want there to be a relationship."

"Why? It seems he has Eli as a father figure."

"But Nate is his father. And he tries, he's just not good at it."

"The best thing for Luke is stability. Is Nate still randomly picking him up?"

"Yes, with no regard to our plans, and it's very spur of the moment."

"Are you looking for financial support?"

"It'd be nice, but not necessary."

"Minnesota has a referee system. It has experts in the field, judges, lawyers, and social workers who work as mediators for these types of things. You can file custody paperwork and Nate has thirty days to respond. You wouldn't have to deal with court or lawyer's fees. You and Nate would sit down and set up an agreement concerning visitation. It's less formal and confrontational, but still as binding as any other legal proceeding."

Jessica scrolled on her phone to locate a few numbers. Writing them down on a piece of paper she handed it to Mary Beth.

"These are a few names of some really good ones. I've even considered taking the classes to be one now that Pete's in school. File the paperwork. The longer you put it off the more Nate can get away with and the harder it is on Luke. He's a great kid, but I can tell when he's seen Nate."

"How?"

"He seems off balance. Not because of something Nate did, just from the disruption in his schedule. You give him stability. That he understands."

"So, I just fill out the papers and file them."

"Pretty much. You can pick your referee or have one assigned. The ones I gave you I know and trust their judgment. They put the child first. Above the wants and desires of the parents."

"That's good. Most days I question if what I'm doing is right for Luke."

"If you didn't you wouldn't be a mom. I'm sure your mom and hers were the same."

"If they did they hid it well."

"Of course, we want our kids to think we're superheroes. Trust me, Luke thinks you're pretty amazing." Jess set down her coffee cup and rested her head on the heel of her hand. "I do have one question. Luke said you broke your friend's hand, a couple of times."

Mary Beth laughed. "That's part of my superpowers. My friend Gabbie has been my catcher for softball for years…I've got a mean fastball. Recently I've come to believe it's due to pent up rage. Eli's been helping me find better ways to release it."

"Oh has he?" Jess raised her eyebrow.

"Not that, although that has been and eye opening experience, too, um…wow…no he…" Mary Beth covered her face that felt aflame. Letting out a cleansing breath she refocused on Jess, who had the biggest smile on her face.

"I'm making you stay for coffee more often, you're a hoot. So, what about Eli is eye opening?"

After dinner Mary Beth went to the Minnesota Department of Justice's webpage and pulled up the papers she'd need to file. While scanning the documents Elias came up behind her and placed his hands on her shoulders. She jumped slightly, and then placed her hand on his.

"Whatcha doing?"

"Jessica told me about a way I could set up a custody arrangement without having to pay a lawyer. I'm just trying to see if I understand any of it."

"Doesn't Case have those types of connections?"

"I don't want to bother him for this. His connections are his father's old business partners."

"Are you trying for full custody?"

"No, just a schedule. I've tried to set one up a few times with Nate before…"

Eli began rubbing a knot out of Mary Beth's shoulder. His hands were so strong and powerful.

"That feels really good," she moaned and dropped her head so he could work his way up her neck. "Thanks for putting him to bed."

"We have a deal. He reads a book and if I don't fall asleep then I get to read one to him. If he withstands both he gets to play for another half hour."

"Is he still up?"

"Has he ever been awake when I put him to bed?"

Good point.

Mary Beth turned around in the chair and faced Eli.

"You got some little kid magic don't you?"

"I have the maturity level of a seven-year-old."

"True." She smiled and he pulled her up. "But it has to be more than that."

"I carry chloroform around with me at all times." Mary Beth wrapped her arms around his neck.

"That's it. I knew you had a trick up your sleeve."

Elias brushed back her hair slightly.

"Are you growing your hair out?"

"It has been a while since I went to the salon. Does it look bad?"

"No, I love long hair."

"Do you?"

"Yes."

"Hmm…someone might have mentioned that to me."

"I'm assuming their last name was Marquez."

"At one time."

"Angelica. Are you growing it out for me?"

"Isn't that what your woman should do?"

"Hmm…so, let's sit down together and look over this paperwork. I'm sure between the two of us we could figure it out."

"You're not too tired? You did have two bedtime stories."

"Being around you keeps me very awake."

Mary Beth looked down and then stepped closer so she could feel how awake he truly was.

"There are a lot of lines to fill out."

"Is it important to you?" he asked as he leaned his forehead against hers.

"Yes, very."

"I can wait."

Mary Beth instantly felt a buzz at the juncture of her sex. How had she gotten so lucky to find a guy willing to put her needs in front of his? Ironically, by doing so, her needs shifted. Her lips found his and he sent her to another place.

"You need to fill out those forms."

"They'll still be there in an hour."

"An hour. I think someone has a very high opinion of me."

Mary Beth snaked her right hand down his stomach to the top of his pants.

"A very high opinion." She smiled as she tugged his waistband, and then turned in his arms.

Elias began to nibble on her neck. The soft bites caused Mary Beth's head to fall back as her eyes closed. She wanted to only use the sensations of touch, taste, and feel with him tonight. She needed his hands to explore her and cause her skin to goose bump.

Popping the buttons of her polo exposed the top of her breasts. Just enough room for her to look down as his hand worked its way up from the bottom of her shirt. The sight of his fingers brushing aside the cotton cup of her bra sent shivers down her back. She'd never been a voyeur, but watching him roll her erect nipple between his thumb and forefinger

147

was as exciting as the feel of it. What else could she watch? Maybe sight wasn't something she wanted to lose.

"You seem fascinated by something, *mi reina*." He then cupped her whole breast and she melted against his body. His other hand wrapped around her waist to keep her upright. "What do you want me to do? Are you going to tell me today? *Mi reina's* been very quiet lately. I fell in love with the woman who demanded I take her. Do I need to tease it out of you? Do I need to bring you to the brink again?"

Eli had begun asking her to describe what she wanted. Up until now she'd kissed him and used her hands, but he was behind her and had a firm hold to her hips. She wouldn't be able to turn around this time. This time he had the upper hand and her body quaked against his.

His hand slid down her belly to the top of her jeans. With a flick of his finger, her top button unhooked and she inhaled sharply. Bending at her waist slightly created a window from her already open polo top. She could see the top of her jeans, her olive green panties, and his hand. It was large in comparison to her hips. She'd never noticed until it was sliding underneath her panties. Her breath quickened as she felt two fingers, one on either side of her clit.

"Elias," she moaned.

"Yes," he growled in her ear. He'd bent the same way she had and she could feel his weight on her back. It was amazing. His hand delved deeper in her pants and all she could see was his wrist as two fingers entered her.

Mary Beth's hand reached behind her and held tight to his neck as he began to stroke her. Agonizingly slow at first. He knew what he was doing and how it was torturing her. But still she bit her tongue. As his speed increased she reached for her couch and dropped to her knees on the cushions. Her legs spread and he added a finger to the extra space allotted to him.

"That's right, I can feel how much you like this. Is this all you want, *mi reina*?"

Sweat beaded on her forehead as she felt a release coming any second now…Elias stopped, removed his fingers, and Mary Beth's head whipped around to stare at him.

"What do you want, *mi reina*?"

"Are you kidding me here?" she panted as every hormone ran around her body looking for somewhere to escape. It was like she had a vice on her clit holding in her orgasm.

"I want you to say it. Let it out."

"What do you want me to let out? My orgasm? You've...oh my God...how would you like me to blow you and stop as your balls began to clench?"

Eli smiled at her. "That's it, get it out. I know what you want, I just want to hear you say it."

"Your dick," she said in a low tone as if she were in a library. "Is that what you want me to say? Eli, I want your dick, now will you please finish what you started?"

Eli locked his hands around her wrists and pressed himself against her ass.

"I'm not a piece of meat," he whispered in her ear, and the tingling focused on her neck. "I want you to tell me how you want it."

"Why?" she whimpered, wishing the ache could go away.

"It'll be freeing. It'll release all that tension in your neck."

"You know what will release all the tension in my body? Your dick inside me as you pound the shit out of my pussy from the back. Is that detailed—"

Elias ripped her pants down to her knees and pressed his cock head against her wanton sex. Oh, God that was what she needed.

"You're so damn sexy when you're frustrated."

She heard a condom wrapper tear and a moment later a violent thrust of his hips filled her to capacity. Instantly she clenched him and he moaned in her ear.

"God you're amazing," he groaned.

It took one slow stroke back, then a hard one for her to come around his cock. But he'd just begun, and as he held tight to her hips he drove himself over and over inside her. Having come so quickly, she didn't get a break. She didn't have three or four orgasms. No, she had one continuous one that lasted for five minutes while he thrust himself hard and fast.

Digging her fingers into the cushion, Mary Beth could only hold on for her life. Every muscle in her body was spent by the time Eli slammed against her hips for the last time and buried himself deep inside, emptying every bit of come he had into her. Her knees wobbled as she fell to the couch and he pulled out. Eli tried to wrap his arms around her, but the sensation was too much and she slapped him away.

"Don't touch me," she sputtered. She wanted to strip naked and float in the air. Everything that touched her body sent a shock wave that made her feel as if she was having convulsions. Holy hell what had he done to her? The tension was very much gone, but she couldn't see straight.

"Are you okay?" he asked her. "I didn't hurt you did I? I didn't mean—"

Mary Beth placed her fingers over his lips to silence him, but even that caused an electric shock to her system.

"You can do whatever you want to me." She tried stretching her body out and contorting. Nothing helped. "That is if I'm ever able to stand up straight."

"I'm assuming I did something good." He laughed.

Mary Beth clutched his shirt and pulled his head to hers until they were nose to nose. She needed him close because she couldn't see past her nose. "You've ruined me for every other man. You can never leave me."

"I'm going to clean up and start looking at those forms. How about you lay here for a little bit?"

"Yeah, good idea."

"Are you relaxed at least?"

"I'm not sure I still have a skeletal structure."

Chapter Thirteen

Throughout life people will make you mad, disrespect you, and treat you bad. Let God deal with the things they do, cause hate in your heart will consume you too.

—Will Smith

"Hey, what's going on, Mary Beth?" Eli asked after dinner.

"I got a call today. The referee I asked for got her response from Nate already and would like to get everything settled before Christmas. Actually, she said something about getting it done so Luke could have a week or two to adapt before the holidays reset everything again."

"Is that a bad thing?"

"No, in theory. Except she had a cancellation on her schedule and can get us in tomorrow. It's too fast. I don't think I'm ready for it."

"Change is always hard."

"I'm buying a building, filling out grant proposals, talking with state agencies every other day. Oh yeah, and failing all my classes. What am I thinking?"

"I thought you got a B on your last stats exam."

"Yeah," Mary Beth said, empathically. "A B. A straight B. Not a B plus and it sure as hell wasn't an A minus."

"Okay, okay," Eli said as he walked behind Mary Beth and began rubbing her tight shoulder muscles. "Remember when we talked about you taking a break?"

"I can't take a break. I'm not a single guy that works for a company that gives vacation days. I'm a mother and business owner and a student. Those things don't get breaks, ever."

Mary Beth was about to start foaming at the mouth. Since Luke had already gone to bed because the pool had obviously knocked him and Mary Beth out before they even got in to eat, Eli knew he'd have to get his tired queen to bed so she could sleep. Sleep and reset her frazzled mind.

"You're right. You have a week before your finals then you'll have one thing off your plate. How about this? I'll take Luke for the next week too."

"What?"

"For the next week I'll take Luke to and from daycare. He can start a little later in the day because I'm not an owner. I'm an employee for another company so I show up at eight."

"School starts at seven-thirty," she snapped.

"I'll drop him off at school then. I'll even talk to my boss about taking a few hours off on Friday and I will be the super mom. You give me his schedule and I'll make it work with mine."

"Why are you doing this?" she growled.

"Because you are a grumpy butt," he said in the most child-like way he could to get her to smile, which thankfully for all involved, she did.

"What else are you going to fix?"

"Well, I figure tomorrow I'll take a few hours and help you with the ref."

"You can't be there. You're not Luke's dad."

The way Mary Beth snarled at him he couldn't help being pissed.

"You're right, I'm not," Eli finally snapped.

He'd had enough. Sure Mary Beth was stressed but that was no reason to turn him into her favorite punching bag. Now he understood why she kept her rage capped. Unfortunately, he'd unleashed the beast who'd been pent up way too damn long and it'd be his job to tame it again. Mary Beth had never had a man she could count on, and right now she was a trapped animal lashing out.

"Don't worry, Mary Beth, you didn't need my help before. I'm sure you'll get through all this fine."

Eli got up and slammed the door as he stalked to his apartment. He wished he didn't feel like he was Luke's dad at times like this. Did she not pay attention to him making them supper while she gave Luke his swimming lesson? Did she miss him giving Luke a bath while she cleaned up the kitchen? Or was it when he spent a half hour reading a chapter book so Luke couldn't fight the sleep in an effort to stay up late.

Eli now helped with homework, discipline, and caring for Luke. He practically lived at Mary Beth's, except for her get-out-of-my-bed-before-Luke-wakes rule. For all intents and purposes, he was Luke's father. God knows Nate wasn't doing anything. Hell, Eli's mother now counted Luke as one of her grandbabies.

As much as he wanted to hate Mary Beth right now and tell her to jump off a bridge, he couldn't. He loved her and the hardest part of being in love was knowing when to give the person you love space. And right now Mary Beth needed about seven miles between her and the world. He just wished he were a part of her and not the world.

* * * *

Mary Beth sat nervously in the room as she waited for the referee to arrive. She wished she hadn't snapped at Eli when he was just trying to be helpful. Right now she wanted him beside her to remind her she didn't have to settle for Nate. She was better than that and, more importantly, she deserved more from life than to be the other woman forever.

Nate came in with Carrie by his side and sat across the table from her.

"I thought it was just supposed to be the two of us?" Mary Beth feared her voice had been too soft for anyone to hear.

"You'd like that wouldn't you?" Carrie sneered, dissuading that fear. "Were you planning on begging him to leave me again? Preying on his love of family. You're pathetic."

Mary Beth felt a headache that hadn't been there for weeks returning. Carrie didn't have a clue. The funny part was, as much as Mary Beth wanted to beat the sense into Carrie, she just felt sorry for her. She'd been her not that long ago. Had she really been that blind? No, she hadn't, and she could tell in Carrie's eyes she wasn't that blind either.

"I'm sorry I'm running a bit behind today," the referee said as she entered the room with an armful of paperwork. "Thank you for your patience. My name is Judge Kolenfloust. Although I'm a judge for these proceedings we are taking things to a more intimate level, so please call me Julie."

"Hello Julie," Mary Beth said as she extended her hand. "Nice to meet you."

Julie shook it and smiled. "You are Mary Beth Wallace, the child in question's mother?"

"Yes."

"And I'm Nathan Schmitz and this is my wife Carrie."

"Okay, so I know the parties involved, let's start with the basics. Mary Beth, Nate, can you tell me a little bit about your son, Lucas."

"You don't want my opinion?" Carrie growled.

"Maybe, let me deal with his parents before I move on to additional parties."

Mary Beth talked about how Luke was in school based on the last parent-teachers conference. His swimming lessons, favorite books, and foods. She told of how he took pride in teaching the younger kids at Growing Strong skills he'd already mastered. Then she told about the time when Zack, a three year old, had scraped his knee and needed a band-aide. Luke had held his hand the whole time and then got him a snack after. Nate nodded in agreement with every word, but didn't add anything new.

"Nate, can you tell me a few things?"

"Um, yeah, it's pretty much like Mary Beth said. He's really smart and stuff. He's not tender hearted like she says though."

"Really, why's that?" Julie queried.

"He's a tough kid."

"A tough kid can't help others?" Julie questioned.

"I'm sure they can, but the whole holding his hand and giving him a hug...my boy doesn't do that kind of stuff." Nate adjusted in the chair and glanced at Mary Beth.

"Not a big hugger?"

"No."

Mary Beth sucked in her breath and turned her head to the window.

"You don't agree, Mary Beth?" Julie's voice made her turn.

"I see a different side of Luke. He always helps the kids at my business and he looks out for the little kids. When he gets off the bus he gives me a hug and tells me all about his day. Every night before he gets his story I get a good night hug and kiss."

She held back the relationship between Luke and Elias. No reason to incite Nate's rage by telling about snuggling on Eli's lap during movie night or the reason she gets hugs before his story was because Eli was the one reading to him now.

"So you're there to put him on and get him off the bus."

"Yes, see when I got pregnant with Luke my friends and I got together and purchased an established daycare center. I couldn't be a stay at home mom like my mother was, but I knew the importance of it. My business partner Amanda suggested it as a way to be there for Luke every day."

"Advice from Mandy," Nate scoffed. "What other tips has she given you?"

"Do you have a problem with Mary Beth's business partners?" Julie asked, and Mary Beth clawed her own leg to keep from jumping up.

"Let's just say that Mary Beth's choice in friends makes me uncomfortable with the way Luke is being raised."

"Not just Amanda? There are others that are questionable?"

"Her best friend Sarah lives an alternative lifestyle."

"What does that mean exactly?" Julie asked.

"Sarah's a lesbian who's lived with her partner for almost two years. She also just completed her Montessori training for the elementary level and will be in charge of our E1 level when our day care is converted into a school."

"The day care you purchased is now becoming a school?" Julie questioned as she raised an eyebrow and scribbled on her yellow legal pad.

"Yes, see, when we first purchased it we started to research other methods of child care and education."

"That must have been hard at eighteen."

"It was, we had...well my friends had savings from their college funds and their parents co-signed the loans. Luckily the previous owner became an employee and helped us with all the rough edges the first year while we completed all of our certifications."

"You just work there then. You're not a partner?"

"My partnership was earned by working. I didn't get paid the first year."

"How did you live?"

"I stayed at a friend's and cooked and cleaned for her family as well as worked nights at Target stocking shelves."

"How long did you do that?"

"I moved in with Gabbie when I was about four months pregnant," Mary Beth said, as her head cocked to the side to make sure the timeline was right. "I stayed until Luke was about two. I stopped working at Target after he was born."

"During this time did Nate help you out?"

"Yes," Nate snapped.

Julie kept her eyes on Mary Beth.

"Nate was traveling a lot, but he did come by when he could." Mary Beth fidgeted as her fingers knitted together.

"In your opinion is Nate a good father?"

Unlocking her fingers Mary Beth played with the pen in front of her. She knew she had enough evidence and examples to limit Nate to almost no visitation, but that wouldn't be fair to Luke. Even with Eli around Nate was Luke's father and he needed that connection. She still hoped Nate would finally step up.

"Nate has the potential to be an amazing dad," she began, and Nate's glare went to a face of confusion. "I see these sparks. He just needs more long-term time with him. Usually he only gets him for a few hours here or there. Never an overnight. Right now he's more of the cool uncle then his dad."

"You want me to have more visitation?" Nate balked.

"Luke needs a schedule. If that schedule gives you a whole weekend, so be it. I don't want the last minute calls saying I need to get Luke to this place or that. Luke and I will have plans we have to scrap because you have three hours free. That's not being a dad. A dad would know Luke is suffering because he doesn't know where he's going to be from day to day. When he gets into a rhythm because you've been busy for a few weeks he relaxes and then he's sitting down to do something and you show up and throw him off."

"Nate, what do you think of what Mary Beth is saying? Can you understand where she's coming from?" Julie asked.

"I don't have a schedule for my life. I do random jobs around the city."

"So, your employment status is?" Julie asked as she moved down her yellow legal pad to make additional notes.

"Unemployed at this time," Nate mumbled.

"What random jobs do you do?"

"Bar back and bounce at various clubs. Occasionally I ump youth baseball games, but I'm the new guy on the block."

"Do you have a future career you're thinking about?"

"He's going to be going to college next year," Carrie chimed in.

Mary Beth had to stop herself from shaking her head. Nate had been going to start college for the past three years.

"What will be your area of study?"

"He's going to be—"

"I asked him." Julie stopped Carrie who leaned back in her chair and crossed her arms. "Nate, what do you plan to study?"

"Plumbing, Carrie says plumbers make a lot of money."

"They do, but what do you want to do?"

"I don't know. One of the guys I bounce with says he could get me on as a guard at the workhouse."

"Working in a prison is a good job. Hard, but good. It will help you conform to a schedule and that could benefit Luke greatly."

"Can I speak?" Carrie asked.

"Yes, please," Julie said.

"How do we know she'll stick to it?" Carrie sneered at Mary Beth.

"I haven't been the issue." Mary Beth tried to control her growl.

"If we set up this schedule and rearrange our life for Luke then there needs to be some concessions on her part."

"Shut up," Nate said as his blue eyes stayed locked on Mary Beth's, but she knew she wasn't the target of his rage this time.

"Don't tell me to—"

"He's my son." Nate turned to Carrie to get her to stop talking. "Mary Beth's right, I haven't been a father."

"Yes you have, baby, you're amazing with him."

"I haven't taken being a father seriously. Can you leave us alone for a few minutes?"

"Me?" Carrie asked.

"You and Julie."

"I don't think that'd be a good idea," Mary Beth said as she began to tremble.

"Do you fear for your safety?" Julie asked.

"No, Nate would never physically hurt me."

"Emotionally?" The kind eyes of the referee reminded Mary Beth there were people out there willing to help. She didn't have to do this on her own.

"Only if I let him. I'll be fine. I'm sorry I protested."

Julie escorted the objecting Carrie out and Mary Beth crossed her arms. She wasn't going to be open to Nate as he sat across the table from her.

"Thank you."

Mary Beth's eyes widened as she pressed her fingers against her ear sure she misheard.

"I'd say you're welcome, but I'm not sure what you're thanking me for."

"Not giving up on me. Most girls would have just kept Luke away from me. There were times I would have never seen him if you didn't make me. Especially early on."

Nate wiped his hand over his face, and then rested his elbows on the table.

"My mom would have let you move in with us, but I didn't want to feel tied down. I never paid attention to how hard you worked when Luke was little. Did Maury really make you cook and clean?"

"I wasn't going to live there rent free. It was the least I could do."

"That must have been draining after working all day."

Mary Beth shifted in her chair unsure of how to respond.

"You know what's funny? I've always seen us together in the end. Old farts sitting on our porch as Luke brought his kids to us. You're who I wanted when I grew up I guess."

"The problem is I grew up first."

"I didn't expect that." Nate leaned on the table bringing himself to her this time. "You've always been mine."

"I love Elias."

"Elias seems like a good guy."

"He is."

"I wish my mom would have tried harder to keep my dad in my life. George is great, but—"

"When you mature past age twelve you're gonna be an awesome dad."

Nate laughed. "I hope so. I read what you put in your petition. I think Carrie stopped at the first line. You were pretty generous."

"You're not a monster no matter what my friends or I say. I knew what I was doing these past few years."

"I knew you didn't want to do it. Not really. You did it because of Luke. You're a pretty good mom, Mary Beth."

"I don't know if sleeping with you makes me a good mom."

"Sacrificing for him does. Look I've been saving some money. It's not much, but—"

"Add it to Luke's college fund," Mary Beth insisted. "I don't need it."

"Luke has a college fund?"

"I'm sure right now it'll cover a credit and a half." She smiled. "But yes, he does."

"Should we call them back in here?"

"Let's you and I set a schedule first."

"We can do that?"

"We could have done that six years ago. The ref will need to approve it, but yeah, we can."

Mary Beth and Nate hammered out a pretty good split of Luke's time. She'd still have him for the majority of time, but now Nate had set times and set parameters. Mary Beth had something better—Nate's respect. He no longer looked at her as someone he could control.

The rest of the proceedings took a fraction of the time Mary Beth thought, and as she walked out of the room, she saw Eli sitting on a wooden bench in the hallway. He was typing away on his laptop and, although he did look up when he heard the door open, he hadn't said a word. As Mary Beth walked over to him he returned to his work.

When she sat he closed his laptop and looked at her.

"You came."

"I came. More for this then what happened in there. You could handle that, this is the part where I thought you might need a hug," Eli said as he scanned her face. "You don't look like you need a hug."

"Need...want...such similar, yet different words."

"You want a hug then?"

"Very much so, and to say I'm sorry. I was tired and..."

"It's okay."

"No, it's not. You are very important to Luke and when I sent him off to school today, he was excited he would get some guy time next week. You're still willing to take him aren't you?"

"Um...I don't have a problem with a week of me and him. But are you sure?"

"I can do a lot on my own, but that's not fair to me or Luke."

Mary Beth held Eli's hands and felt the warmth she'd been missing in the conference room. She'd wanted to hold on to Eli while she worked things out with Nate. Her leg had to be purple from how hard she dug her fingers in during parts of the negotiation, especially in the beginning.

"Thank you. When I saw you sitting here, let's just say I was dizzy again."

"I do tend to make you lightheaded a lot, don't I?"

"Actually, I've been thinking about that. When I'm with you the headaches are gone. I think this might be reality and I just don't understand it since it's been so long."

"I take away your pain, huh?" Eli smiled and Mary Beth brought her forehead to his.

"*Muchísimo, mi rey.*"

Epilogue

The family you come from isn't as important as the family you're going to have.

—Ring Lardner

One Year Later

With three quick knocks on Mary Beth's door, Elias steeled himself. He'd seen Luke sitting on the steps for a half hour before Mary Beth brought him inside. Sure, he was using the situation to his advantage and he should be ashamed, but he wasn't in the least.

"Hey, Eli," Mary Beth said as she opened the door. "I wasn't expecting you tonight. It might not be the best time—"

Eli held his hand up to silence her.

"How many?" he asked.

"Four," she said, holding up four fingers.

Nate hadn't shown up for his visit for the fourth time in a row. Eli was sure he hadn't called either.

"Well, I'm not here to see you."

"You're not?" She smiled as she leaned against her doorjamb.

"No," Eli replied as he kissed her lightly on the cheek and entered the apartment. "At least not right now."

"It better be not right now," she said as she squeezed his ass.

"Woman," he growled, and she turned into the kitchen to finish cooking supper. "Hey, Lucas Maximus."

161

"Hey, Eli," Luke grumbled as he hugged tighter to the throw pillow and leaned on the arm of the couch. His face was downturned even though the TV was on with his favorite cartoon.

"Luke, I need to talk to you man to man. You up for that?"

Luke turned his face up to Eli. "I'm not a man."

"You're the man of this house, sorta. Either way I need to ask for your blessing on something."

"What's a blessing?"

"It's like saying it's okay for me to do something because you think it's a good idea."

"Why do I need to be a man?"

"I want to do something really big that will change your life."

"Mine?" Luke was becoming more interested and sat up a little.

"Yours."

"What is it?"

"I want to ask your mom to marry me."

"Marry her? How would that change my life?"

"We'd all live in the same house and I'd be your stepdad."

"Could I still call you Eli?"

"What else would you call me?"

"You gonna want a baby?" Luke grumbled as he held the pillow tighter to his chest.

"I don't want to lie to you and say no because I'm sure eventually we might want another great kid like you."

"If I'm so great why you want another baby? Why am I not enough?"

That backfired. Eli steeled himself and adjusted. He'd gotten used to Luke's mood swings over the last few months.

"I never said you weren't. I just think it'd be cool to have two of you." Eli ran his fingers through Luke's hair and then patted him on the shoulder. "I know it's been hard since baby Gemma was born for you to get time with your dad, but you and I get along right?"

"Yeah."

"And you live with your mom."

"So. You could still forget about me."

"I can't forget about you when I'm at work, or visiting my mom or even when your mom and I go out alone. How could I forget about you when you're sitting across the table from me at dinner and sleeping across the hall?"

"You think about me when you're working?"

"All the time. I'll start laughing remembering something silly you said or did and they all look at me like I'm crazy."

"Why do you need my…what did you call it?"

"Blessing, because I'd be asking you to share your mom and for your mom to share you. I wouldn't be your cool neighbor any more, I'd be another dad."

"If I say no what are you gonna do? You gonna not come around anymore?"

"I guess I have to wait until you say yes."

"Yes to what?" Mary Beth came over to them and sat on the arm of the chair Eli was sitting in.

She looked from Eli to Luke and back again.

"What did I miss?"

"Eli wants to marry you," Luke stated plainly.

"Luke, I was going to ask her all romantic like. You're killing my game."

"Sorry," he grumbled. "It's not like you have much anyway."

Mary Beth's jaw had dropped slightly, but she quickly recovered as she swallowed hard. Eli placed his hand on her knee and she clutched his hand.

"I'm trying to get Luke's permission to ask you."

"You were? And what did he say?"

They both looked at Luke whose eyebrows were knitted together, and Eli wanted to alleviate the pressure on him.

"I shouldn't have asked him. I'm sorry to put all this on your shoulders."

"I like that you asked me," Luke's blue eyes smiled at Eli. "Nobody asks me nothing, but you do. And I like that. I just wanted you to say I had to call you dad."

"I was hoping you'd do that on your own."

Luke got up and wrapped his arms around Eli's neck. The warmth of the small boy made Eli's heart skip a beat. Returning the hug Eli looked over his shoulder at Mary Beth.

"I guess that's settled," she said as she gasped a bit for breath.

"Not yet, *mi reina,* but now I'll have to figure out how to surprise you with a proposal fit for a queen." He tapped Luke's back to get him to release his grip. "I was hoping to surprise your mama."

Mary Beth crawled onto his lap and laid herself across him with her legs dangling over the arm of the chair. "Never in my dreams would I have ever envisioned a better proposal than the one I just saw."

Eli leaned his forehead on hers, losing himself in the green speckles dotting her eyes.

"Are you to gonna kiss?" Luke asked with a bit of disgust.

"Every chance we get," Mary Beth confirmed. "That's what married folk do."

"That a yes, *mi reina?"*

"I don't think yes is a big enough word to accept your proposal."

Capturing her lips, Eli fell into his woman and, just like the first time, he looked into her eyes and saw forever.

About the Author

Michel Prince is an author who graduated with a bachelor degree in History and Political Science. Michel writes young adult and adult paranormal romance as well as contemporary romance.

With characters yelling "It's my turn, damn it!!!" She tries to explain to them that alas, she can only type a hundred and twenty words a minute and they will have wait their turn. She knows eventually they find their way out of her head and to her fingertips and she looks forward to sharing them with you.

When Michel can suppress the voices in her head she can be found at a scouting event or cheering for her son in a variety of sports. She would like to thank her family for always being in her corner, and especially her husband for supporting her every dream and never letting her give up.

Michel has been awarded Elite Status with Rebel Ink Press in 2013, the service award for her local RWA chapter Midwest Fiction Writers in 2013 and 2014, won Sweetest Romance at IREA and is a PAN member of RWA. She lives in the Twin Cities with her husband, son, and dog, Bolt.

You may contact the author at:

www.michelprincebooks.com
www.facebook.com/michelprincebooks
https://twitter.com/michelprince1

www.ingramcontent.com/pod-product-compliance
Lightning Source LLC
Chambersburg PA
CBHW052136170626
46812CB00004B/1459